BLOODY SUNRISE

*The EDGE series by George G. Gilman
available from New English Library:*

EDGE 1: THE LONER
EDGE 2: TEN THOUSAND DOLLARS AMERICAN
EDGE 3: APACHE DEATH
EDGE 4: KILLER'S BREED
EDGE 5: BLOOD ON SILVER
EDGE 6: THE BLUE, THE GREY AND THE RED
EDGE 7: CALIFORNIA KILLING
EDGE 8: SEVEN OUT OF HELL
EDGE 9: BLOODY SUMMER
EDGE 10: VENGEANCE IS BLACK
EDGE 11: SIOUX UPRISING
EDGE 12: THE BIGGEST BOUNTY
EDGE 13: A TOWN CALLED HATE
EDGE 14: THE BIG GOLD
EDGE 15: BLOOD RUN
EDGE 16: THE FINAL SHOT
EDGE 17: VENGEANCE VALLEY
EDGE 18: TEN TOMBSTONES TO TEXAS
EDGE 19: ASHES AND DUST
EDGE 20: SULLIVAN'S LAW
EDGE 21: RHAPSODY IN RED
EDGE 22: SLAUGHTER ROAD
EDGE 23: ECHOES OF WAR
EDGE 24: THE DAY DEMOCRACY DIED
EDGE 25: VIOLENCE TRAIL
EDGE 26: SAVAGE DAWN
EDGE 27: DEATH DRIVE
EDGE 28: EVE OF EVIL
EDGE 29: THE LIVING, THE DYING AND THE DEAD
EDGE 30: WAITING FOR A TRAIN
EDGE 31: THE GUILTY ONES
EDGE 32: THE FRIGHTENED GUN
EDGE 33: THE HATED
EDGE 34: A RIDE IN THE SUN
EDGE 35: DEATH DEAL
EDGE 36: TOWN ON TRIAL
EDGE 37: VENGEANCE AT VENTURA
EDGE 38: MASSACRE MISSION
EDGE 39: THE PRISONERS
EDGE 40: MONTANA MELODRAMA
EDGE 41: THE KILLING CLAIM
EDGE 42: BLOODY SUNRISE

EDGE MEETS ADAM STEELE: TWO OF A KIND
EDGE MEETS ADAM STEELE: MATCHING PAIR

BLOODY
SUNRISE

George G. Gilman

NEW ENGLISH LIBRARY

for:

B.L.
who rode for a lot of other
outfits before he joined this
one.

_____

A New English Library Original Publication,
1982

Copyright © 1982 by George G. Gilman

First NEL Paperback Edition September 1982

NEL Books are published by
New English Library,
Mill Road, Dunton Green,
Sevenoaks, Kent,
a division of Hodder & Stoughton Ltd.

Made and printed in Great Britain by
Hunt Barnard Ltd., Aylesbury, Bucks.

British Library Cataloguing in Publication Data

Gilman, George G.
    Bloody sunrise.—(Edge; 42)
    Rn: Terry Harknett   I. Title   II. Series
    823'.914[F]   PR6058.A686/

    ISBN 0-450-05505-1

One

THE slow riding lone horseman first saw the two figures on the south bank of the Sweetwater when he was still several miles to the north of the river. Then lost sight of them and had them in view again by irregular turns as he allowed the bay gelding to make his own pace down through the foothills of the Green Mountains in central Wyoming Territory. Following a trail that had been well used long ago but lately was little travelled.

For more than an hour after the initial sighting, the pair in the river valley made no move that was visible over such a distance as they lay sprawled on their backs at the base of a grassy knoll. Apparently asleep in the bright, warm sunlight of early afternoon. Then one of the men spotted the approaching rider skylined against the cloudless blue on a high granite ridge, and folded up off his back, stared and fisted grit from his eyes and stared again. Only when he was certain of what he saw did he reach out to shake his partner awake. This man started to go through the same series of actions to verify that somebody was riding down out of the mountains, but before his sleep blurred vision cleared, the horseman had moved off the ridge and his silhouette was lost in a patch of deep shade. Still following the tortuous foothills trail that nobody else had found reason to use for a very long time.

The rider, whose name was Edge, murmured to his mount who had no name: 'You figure those two fellers are the reason nobody comes this way anymore?'

He spoke his thought aloud to the unresponsive horse as the two men rose stiffly from where they had been sleeping in the sun and ambled into a small timber shack on the other side of the trail that curved around and ran from sight beyond the grassy knoll: closed the door and did not re-emerge. But perhaps continued to seek another glimpse of the man in the foothills from the glassless window in the river facing side wall of the shack. But such a sighting could not be made for close to thirty minutes, for man and mount were down behind an elongated rise before they came through a curved ravine to start across the gentle slope that was the western side of the river valley.

And Edge knew he was under close observation as he rode down the grade pasture toward the river crossing point about a mile and a half away – saw the glint of sunlight against the lens of a telescope that was trained upon him from out of the shadow behind the window of the shack.

This effect of bright light striking a polished surface maybe as sharp as the glint in the eyes of the man called Edge. Ice blue eyes that were permanently narrowed under hooded lids. In a lean face with high cheekbones, a hawklike nose, a thin lipped mouth and a firm jaw. The skin stained darkly by heritage and the elements, and inscribed with deep lines that were caused as much by the harsh experiences of his years as by their number, which was almost forty. Framing this face that might be considered handsome or ugly – determined by how people regarded the stamp of latent cruelty suggested by the narrowed eyes and set of the lips – was a mane of jet black hair worn long enough to brush the shoulders. Mostly black, too, with just a sprinkling of grey, was the more than half a day of stubble that sprouted on his lower face and neck. This grew just a little thicker and longer in the shape of a Mexican style moustache, which was the only adornment affected by Edge: whose face without it anyway would blatantly advertise the fact that there was Latin blood in his veins.

It was his father who was Mexican. His mother was from Scandinavia.

Anyone who did not know Edge could assume that the circlet of dull coloured wooden beads threaded on a leather thong and worn around his neck was an ornament. Whereas it served the purpose of holding in place, between his shoulders at the nape of his neck, a sheath in which was carried a straight razor: more often than not the constantly sharply honed blade used simply for shaving.

The rest of what the six feet three inches tall half breed wore amounted to a conventional outfit of a man riding Western trails. A black Stetson, a grey shirt, blue denim pants with the cuffs hanging outside spurless black boots. Around his waist a brown leather gunbelt with a Frontier Colt in the holster tied down to his right thigh. A bullet in every belt loop.

He sat astride a Western saddle hung with two bags and two canteens. A Winchester jutted from the forward slung boot. Tied on behind the saddle was a bedroll packed with cooking and eating utensils and with a sheepskin coat lashed to the top.

All his clothing and his gear had seen better days. His mount, too, which was a bay gelding with a recently healed bullet wound just below the point of the left shoulder. But the animal was patently well cared for by a rider who knew how to pace a horse over a long trail.

A trail which was now interrupted by the fifty feet width of the Sweetwater. A river that, swollen by melted snow in spring, could be a much wider and deeper torrenting obstacle judging by the tree and rock debris scattered over a wide strip to either side. But today the river flowed slowly and smoothly, with the rocky bed visible for most of its width through the crystal clear water: from where Edge sat his reined in mount, allowing the horse to dip his head and drink while he directed his narrow eyed gaze across the sun sparkled surface toward the shack. In which there was not a sign of life, and had not been ever since he was far enough advanced across the open slope for the watchers to see him clearly without need of the spyglass.

Then he shifted his attention to left and right, scanning the river up and downstream and checking for movement on the less open eastern slope of the valley. But a flock of birds, very high and flying in a south west direction was the only activity in the immediate area: until the gelding was through drinking and Edge heeled him into the river. Like before, letting the horse set his own pace and also, like before, maintaining an apparently nonchalent attitude in the saddle while in fact he was prepared to respond in an instant should the situation become dangerous – to draw the Colt or slide the Winchester from the boot, turn or stop the gelding, remain astride the saddle or power out of it, kill a man – or two – if that was what was required to protect himself.

In midstream for ten feet.or so, the water was deep enough to wet his boots and a few inches of his pants legs: soaked through the fabric to cool his skin which acted to dry the sweat of tension that had erupted at the small of his back.

The sun on its decline toward the Rockies was not hot enough to open a man's pores unless he was exerting himself, but Edge felt no sense of shame that fear drew beads of salt moisture from him again as he neared the far bank of the river. For a man who lived as he did without experiencing fear would have to be an imbecile. Whereas this man accepted it readily and controlled it so that it could be used to heighten his readiness.

'Hold it, stranger!'

'You ride up outta that river and you'll be trespassin'! Unless you got the five dollar price of admission, that is?'

The shack was some forty feet back from the riverside where Edge reined in the gelding – above and beyond the debris marked flood line of the Sweetwater. The man who ordered him to halt swung into view from the left of the glassless window and aimed a Winchester rifle from the shoulder. A hatless, check shirted man with red curly hair and a round face with black button eyes and a smooth, deeply tanned skin. About twenty-five years old, lacking confidence and sweating a great deal more than Edge.

A head shorter than his six feet tall partner who opened the shack door without haste to step outside and offer the explanation. This man of an age with Edge, with a lanky build and a mournful face. Blond haired and pale skinned, the lightness of his colouring emphasised by the all black clothing he wore – recently laundered and pressed clothing styled for smartness rather than durability. Cut on Western lines but only for effect. He aimed his Winchester from the waist which had no gunbelt around it – holding it out to the side as if he was afraid the rifle was oily and might stain his shirt. But he was not afraid of anything else at this time. Met and held the steady gaze of Edge with an unblinking stare that indicated the man was totally indifferent about the outcome of this situation.

'Admission to what?' the half breed asked in an even tone that matched that of the man out front of the shack.

'Elgin County, mister. Property of Mr Earl Gray who don't like to have strangers roamin' his land unless they've paid for the privilege.'

Edge nodded. 'Something I don't like, feller, is to have guns aimed at me.'

The man all in black raised his shoulders about a half inch and dropped them. Asked: 'Who does?'

'Give folks the one warning. If anybody points a gun at me after I've told them not to, they either kill me with it or I kill them.'

Now the man in black nodded. 'Guess everybody has somethin' that gets their backs up, mister. My buddy at the window there, Bob Lowell, he just hates roaches. Can't abide them things. Me, I get itchy skin whenever I come up against tough talkin' saddletramps who figure I'm easy meat just because I take care over the way I look.'

'That's Gabe Millard, stranger!' Lowell said

quickly. 'The gunfighter from Dodge City! Gabe's killed more men than anyone else works for Mr Gray!'

'I'm not of a boastful nature myself, mister,' Millard explained. 'Not much of a talker on any subject, really. Runnin' out of things to say now as a matter of fact.' He altered his expression slightly from indifference to boredom as he motioned with the rifle to left and right. Went on: 'Elgin County stretches twenty miles to north and south of this trail, mister. And you can ride the detour in either direction if you want. Or go back the way you came if you ain't got anythin' much to do in Elgin or beyond. Or you can pay the five dollar toll and have the run of the county.'

'Or you can try to ride on through without payin' the money!' Lowell put in eagerly, much more confident now, 'and pay with your life!'

'Don't pay no mind to Bob, mister,' Millard said. 'He reads a lot.'

Edge heeled the gelding forward from the river side and on to the start of the trail that was heavily imprinted with sign – of wagons and teams that had come down the east slope of the valley, turned between the grassy knoll and the shack and gone back up the grade again.

The black clad man continued to keep his rifle aimed with a mixture of indifference for the target and fastidious concern that the gun should not dirty his clothes.

While his younger partner thrust his Winchester further through the window in an attitude of aggression. And demanded:

'You gonna pay, stranger?'

Edge delved into a pocket of his shirt as he rode

along the centre of the trail, the gelding dripping water that was immediately soaked up by the dusty covering and hard packed soil beneath. Brought out the makings and waited until he reined in the horse again, still in a position to be covered by both repeaters, before he started to form the cigarette. Then asked:

'The five bucks buy me anything other than a short cut, Millard?'

'No, mister.'

'So if I run into more of Gray's hired guns in Elgin County I can get shaken down again?'

'No, you just have to pay the once,' Lowell answered quickly and withdrew from the window. His footfalls rapped on the boarding of the single room shack and the man in black motioned with his head to indicate that they should wait for him to come outside. Which he did, with a roll of two inch wide tickets: minus his rifle. 'You get one of these stranger. Which'll show anyone that asks that you paid the toll to cross Mr Gray's land.'

He extended the roll forward in one hand and prepared to tear off one of the four inch long, white coloured tickets: an enquiring look on his youthful face. Edge angled the cigarette from a side of his mouth and nodded as he reached into a hip pocket, withdrew a roll of bills and found a five spot among them. Replaced the roll and extended the bill.

'I'll take one, feller.'

'Hot damn, that's the first sale been made on this route for best part of two months, I reckon,' Lowell blurted as he came forward with a broad grin splitting his round face.

Millard scowled and rasped a soft voiced obscenity as he side stepped to keep the younger man out of the line of fire.

Edge smiled with his mouth – his ice blue eyes totally devoid of warmth – as he allowed the bill to be taken from his brown skinned hand and accepted the torn off ticket in exchange. Briefly shifted his gaze from the now grimacing face of Gabe Millard to read the legend printed on the ticket:

Paid the amount of $5 which allows bearer to travel freely in Elgin County, Wyoming. By order of Mayor Earl Gray, Elgin City, Elgin County.

'It's a shit job anyway, on this friggin' trail,' the disconcerted Millard growled, seeking to mask his lapse into nervousness. 'Ain't nothin' up in them mountains for anybody to use the trail. Hey, what the hell, mister?'

He had allowed the Winchester to droop so that it was aimed at the ground after the ticket was purchased: as he motioned with his head toward the rugged high ground west of the lush river valley. Now froze and showed an expression of shock that was as wide eyed as that on the face of Lowell. This sudden change brought about by the sight of Edge setting fire to the folded over ticket.

The ticket flared in his left hand as the match was dropped from the right – which streaked to drape the butt of the holstered Colt when Millard made to rake his rifle up and around. The man froze again, as Lowell merely looked down at his holstered revolver, not daring to even twitch a finger toward it.

'That's fine, fellers,' the half breed said evenly. And touched the flaming ticket to his cigarette. Then blew it out before letting go of it. 'One more time and somebody dies.'

'So okay,' Millard countered in an indifferent tone with a matching expression and the slight shrug of his shoulders again.

'I'll give you another pass,' Lowell suggested. 'Or else nobody'll know you paid the toll and –'

'I'll know, feller,' Edge cut in.

'Uh?'

'Got respect for other people's property and if Gray has title to Elgin County I figure he has a right to charge strangers who want to cross his land. And I figure it's worth five bucks to me to avoid having to make the kind of detour this feller spoke of.'

Lowell was impatient for the half breed to be through. And spoke quickly when he had finished.

'But how will anybody know you paid unless you show the pass?'

'Have to take my word,' Edge answered, moving his right hand away from the butt of the Colt to join the left on the reins. Then tapped his heels to the flanks of the gelding.

'Shit, Gabe,' Lowell said bitterly. 'The first pass been sold on this route for all that time and it has to be to a troublemaker!'

'He ain't made no trouble for us, Bob,' the man in black pointed out as both of them gazed after the slow riding half breed. 'We done what we was supposed to.'

The younger man remained anxious. Then abruptly pressed the roll of tickets to his chest with a forearm as he cupped his hands to his mouth to form a bullhorn. And yelled:

'Hey, stranger?'

Edge halted the gelding and turned in the saddle to look back to where Lowell stood out front of the shack while Millard went inside, growling that he was going to fix some coffee.

'They're gonna love you in Elgin City!' the young

man warned bitterly after he failed to think of any kind of plea that might appeal to the half breed.

The rider faced front again and set the gelding moving. Was too far off for his wryly spoken words to carry back to the shack when he murmured:

'Yeah, I wow them in Peoria, too.'

Two

THE eastern side of the river valley was formed of a mixture of grassland, rock outcrops and timber stands: and its incline was steeper than the opposite slope. So the trail made many looping turns toward the crest of the rise to take account of the grade and to bypass obstacles. Its line planned so that wagons could negotiate the valley side without too much difficulty. A horse and rider could have halved the time and distance to the top by taking cut-offs between the switchback turns but Edge elected to steer the gelding along the trail all the way from the river to the tree clad ridge. In no rush to get there – or to anywhere beyond.

Below, smoke began to curl from the chimney of the shack beside the Sweetwater. And above, a wagon with a two horse team in the traces showed briefly on the ridge before the intervening terrain hid it.

The only bird in the sky now was a hawk, soaring very high against the infinite of darkening blue – totally free of all strictures save those imposed by natural instincts and not yet hungry enough to descend and hover in search of food. Edge smoked the cigarette and sat easy in the saddle, contented with his lot as he remained effortlessly alert to his surroundings: his posture and impassive features revealing nothing about what he was thinking.

Which was how the two men on a freshly creosoted buckboard saw him as they came down a curving slope on the fringe of a stand of pine and the half breed rode up the incline. Men who looked much more like tough line riders for a powerful and over possessive landowner than did Gabe Millard and Bob Lowell. Both of them about thirty-five, tall and broad shouldered – soft in the area of their beer bellies maybe but nowhere else. Hard, square cut faces set with small, mean eyes and mouths shaped by the almost permanent scowls that seemed to be part of the uniform of such hired guns: along with the dark garb that was much the worse for wear and holstered revolvers that were never new and were the objects of greater attention than anything else in the restricted lives of such men. These two were recently washed up and shaved and the lack of bristles and dirt on their faces acted somehow to emphasise the mood of sullenness in which they were both sunk.

The one with the reins had blue eyes and long bushy sideburns of black hair – and a staccato vocal delivery when he demanded:

'You buy a pass off Gabe and the kid, Mac?'

'They made sure I did, feller.'

The driver reined in the team and spat a globule of saliva to the side, in the path of the bay gelding. And Edge halted his mount.

'You reach the city before sundown, you'll get more than your money's-worth, Mac,' the passenger on the buckboard drawled in a deep Southern accent. He had a squint in one dark coloured eye and the yellow stained teeth of an inveterate tobacco chewer. Was chewing a plug now, and ran his shirt sleeved left arm across his mouth to wipe away a trickle of juice that was spilled when he spoke. 'Me and Chris are sure sick that we gotta miss seein' the show.'

This man was entirely concerned with his disappointment and now ignored Edge to gaze resentfully into the middle distance directly ahead of the stalled buckboard and team. While Chris peered fixedly at the half breed with a similar expression as he warned:

'If you figure you're a hard man, Mac, you've come to the right neck of the woods to find out how wrong you can be.'

'Is there anything else the five dollars buys me, feller?'

'Uh?'

'Except for permission to cross Elgin County, a show in town and lessons about how I'm maybe not what I think I am?'

Chris deepened the lines of his scowl and spat again, his saliva hitting precisely the stain in the dust left by the earlier globule. And jerked his head to indicate that Edge should continue on up the slope as he rapped out:

'I can see what you think you are, Mac. See it in the way you look and hear it in how you talk. Ain't no maybe about it. And if you head into Elgin City, you best act more respectful. Or you could wind up part of the show.'

'Bear in mind what Chris just told you, Mac,' the other man urged, to reveal that he was aware of what was happening close by while he continued to reflect sourly on more interesting events scheduled to take

18

place at a distance. 'Mr Gray's got a real bad temper and – '

'Quit it, Sam,' Chris growled as he flicked the reins and released the brake to set the buckboard rolling down the slope. 'Figure he's got the message from us if he didn't get it from Gabe and the kid.'

'Told him in black and white, Chris.'

Chris scowled back over his shoulder at Edge who now removed the cigarette butt from his lips and dropped it to the trail – turned just his head to grin coldly at the driver of the rig and said evenly against the creak of timber, rattle of wheel-rims and clop of hooves:

'Don't know about black and white, fellers. Seems I've moved into a Gray area.'

Chris could not have heard the wry comment but he certainly saw the grin and he shook his head – as if to convey that he had tried his best to achieve something but was now prepared to admit failure – before he gave his full attention to steering the buckboard down the snaking slope of the trial. And Edge moved off again in the opposite direction, impassive once more and experiencing total peace of mind in back of the emotionless façade.

Some thirty minutes later he was at the top of the slope and halted the gelding where the trail ran into the extensive expanse of fir trees. Looked down into the valley and saw that the buckboard had been turned around at the shack. Millard and Lowell were up on the seat now, taking their leave of the tobacco chewing Sam and the staccato voiced Chris.

The sloping ground on the other side of the sluggishly flowing Sweetwater River was as deserted as it apparently almost always was, and the valley to north and south was totally lacking in visible life for as far as the slit eyed gaze of the half breed could reach.

The hawk was gliding smoothly toward the rock ridges of the mountains beyond the foothills and then was lost to sight against the sun that was still high enough to be yellow and to dazzle the naked eye with its glare.

Edge turned his back on all this and heeled the gelding along the trail through the timber, where the aromatic air struck cool to his skin. The horse on a loose rein maintained the same unhurried pace as before over ground that was level now. While the half breed kept an apparently casual watch ahead and to either side: relied upon his hearing to warn him of when Millard and Lowell got close enough on his backtrail to merit attention. Which did not happen until he rode out of the three mile wide strip of firs to emerge on a broad, gently rolling plain dotted with homesteads to the north of the arrow straight trail, while the land to the south was cattle range behind a four strand barbed wire fence. Fencing also stretched southward along the fringe of timber.

Widely scattered bunches of healthy looking longhorns grazed the lush pastureland behind the fences. While men and some women worked in the rich soil fields around the small frame houses and barns on the other side of the trail: hoeing, ploughing or drilling. Here and there, smoke from a stove curled out of a chimney and an occasional window gleamed with lamplight as the day faded into evening. And more fires and lamps were lit in the time it took the half breed to roll a cigarette as he listened to the approach of the buckboard on the trail through the timber. The sky noticeably darkened and the air cooled at the same rate, bringing the homesteaders out of the fields and into the houses and causing Edge to take his sheepskin coat from the top of his bedroll and put it on. This as, in the far distance, a faint yellow light formed a dome shape on the eastern horizon: a lot less intense than the staining of red which the setting sun left in its wake above treetops to the south west.

Then full night swooped down fast as the glow of sunset was extinguished. Which made the home-steaders' lamps gleam more brightly and intensified the aura which the lights of Elgin City emanated into the sky.

Edge lit his cigarette as the buckboard, driven by the youthful Lowell, rolled out of the firs and the funereal faced Gabe Millard signalled for the rig to be stopped alongside the man astride the gelding. The blue, glittering light of a three-quarter moon enabled each man to see the others clearly.

'That's the city up ahead, mister,' Millard said.

'What I figured.'

'Land behind the fence is Mayor Gray's Triple X Ranch. Fenced to keep the cows from strayin' on to the crops. High yield soil in Elgin County.'

'Saw the places before nightfall. Looked good.'

'Everythin's good here, mister. Life in general, if folks abide by the rules.'

'I paid already.'

Millard nodded. 'And had to make a point of showin' Bob and me what a hardnose you reckon you are. Same as you acted with Chris Hite and Sam Tufts. You keep on like that in the city and you'll really wish you held on to the five bucks and rode around the county.'

'Nice of you fellers to worry about me so much.'

Lowell vented a scornful grunt as he turned up the

21

collar of his duster then jerked his Stetson harder on to his head.

Millard, who wore a stylishly cut frock coat that added to his funereal appearance, gave one of his slight shrugs and explained: 'Bob and Chris and Sam and me don't give a turd about your hide, mister. But Mayor Gray, he likes things to run smooth in Elgin County. If they don't, then whoever stirs the shit gets his ass kicked. Mostly all the way to hell. But more than likely, it don't end there. On account of it takes the mayor's temper a whole lot longer to cool than it does to get hot. And then life ain't good at all for anybody has to have dealin's with him. Let's roll, Bob.'

'I'll try not to rile – '

'You're a natural born troublemaker in a place like Elgin, mister!' Millard snapped, and extended a hand to hold back Lowell from setting the rig moving. 'And there ain't no doubt in my mind but that you'll stir the shit and get yourself killed and have Mayor Gray mad for a friggin' month . . . .'

'But?' Edge suggested after several seconds of silence when Millard wrenched his gaze away from the face of the half breed to stare angrily toward the dome of light above Elgin.

'Your name Edge?' Lowell asked.

'Right in one, feller.'

'Didn't I say so?' Millard snapped at his partner. 'And didn't Hite say I was right?'

The half breed continued to be impassive and unblinking as he regularly drew against the cigarette and allowed the smoke to trickle out through his nostrils. And his tone remained even when he asked:

'I meet you fellers somewhere I've forgotten about?'

'No, mister. Ain't nobody in the whole county ever come across you before, far as I know. But Mayor Gray, he claims he has good reason to want to meet you.'

'You sure you mean good and not bad, feller?'

'Shit, stranger, Gabe didn't mean awhile back that Mr Gray wants you dead. Not at all. No, Gabe just has it fixed in his mind that a man like you won't do like Mr Gray wants you to.'

'He could be right, feller,' Edge answered. 'Usually aim to do only what I want to do.'

Millard sighed out of his anger and moved his shoulders in a more emphatic shrug than usual. Said quickly: 'Look, mister, Earl Gray figures he has reason to be grateful to you for somethin' that happened years ago. I got no idea what it was. Just seen a drawin' of you in uniform on an old wanted flyer. All of us that work for the mayor have seen it. After you left the shack by the river I kept tryin' to figure out why you looked so familiar to me. And then Chris Hite and Sam Tufts came to take over from me and Bob. And Chris said he got the same feelin' about you. Together, we hit on it. The old wanted flyer that Earl Gray showed us. With the picture of you, a lot younger.'

'About ten years or so,' Edge said reflectively. Then asked quickly when Millard motioned for Lowell to start the buckboard rolling: 'If the top man around here figures he owes me, why are you fellers so anxious I might rub him up the wrong way?'

'You said it just now, mister. That you aim to do what you want to do. And in Elgin County, folks do only what Earl Gray wants them to. Say no to him and the only man around that's happy is Sam Gower.'

'Sam Gower does all the buryin' for the county,' Lowell explained.

'Told you as much as we can, mister,' Millard assured. 'Warned you some about what you can expect. Can't tell you to get the hell outta the county without goin' through town in the event it ever got back to the mayor you was here and we never told him about it. Rest you gotta find out for yourself. And me and Bob and Chris and Sam would be grateful if you didn't let it be known any of us recognised you. So that when the trouble comes, none of us gets extra blame for spottin' who you were. Let's go, Bob. This time for sure.'

Both of them pointedly avoided looking at Edge: as if they were worried that he could force them to remain with a look or a sign. And Lowell yelled at the horses in the traces and with voice and reins commanded a noisy gallop that would serve to cover any question the half breed might ask to delay them.

The sudden lurch forward into high speed raised a cloud of swirling dust from beneath pumping hooves and spinning wheels: and Edge cracked his eyes to the narrowest of slits and compressed his lips until the motes began to settle. Then he struck a match on the stock of the Winchester jutting from the boot and relit the half smoked cigarette before he set the gelding moving in the wake of the racing buckboard. But at a more sedate pace.

The horse snorted and then sneezed.

Edge held the cigarette between two fingers while he licked his lips and spat to the side. Murmured as he angled the smoke from a side of his mouth again: 'Let's go get us something to lay the dust. And hope that in Earl Gray country we can get something stronger than tea.'

Three

EDGE knew he was expected in Elgin City even before he rode off the open trail and on to the broad main street of the prosperous looking community sited in the fold of two low hills beyond the range and homesteader country. For he could sense interested eyes peering out into the moonlit night at him from the moment he was able to see the place, instead of just the glow in the sky from its many lights.

He reached this point on the trail as it made a gentle turn around the base of one of the rises that flanked the town. The last homestead was behind him then and an extensive stand of pinyon was spread out to the north of the trail. While to the south the barbed wire fence had given way to a wooden one, painted white, which guarded the neat lawns and symmetrical plantings that surrounded a hilltop mansion. A stone built, green roofed, three storeyed house with diamond leaded windows and a pillared porch. A broad driveway surfaced with gravel made two graceful curves from an arched gap in the fence to the foot of a set of shallow steps that rose to a balustraded terrace out front of the house, in back and to the sides of which was an arc of pinyon. Every one of the score or so windows on the façade of the house gleamed with lamplight.

Fixed to the arch from where the driveway started there was a pair of horns too large to be real and so probably carved from wood, and hanging from the tips by lengths of chain a sign branded with the legend: EARL GRAY'S TRIPLE X RANCH.

A quarter mile or so from this entrance to the home of the man who claimed to own an entire county in the Territory of Wyoming was Elgin City. Where, he knew, a great many pairs of eyes watched him with intrigued curiosity as he rode the gelding along the curve of the trail between the gleaming white fence and the deeply shadowed expanse of timber. Then past a marker where the fence and the trees ended – branded in the same style as the sign at the entrance to the Triple X – that proclaimed:

EARL GRAY WELCOMES
YOU TO
ELGIN CITY
Elev: 4050   Pop: 2000

A town with an arrow straight main street that was about three-quarters of a mile long and a section of the west to east trail. With, halfway along, curving between the flanking hills to the south, a narrower street with several spurs to either side of its more than a mile length. Every building lining the main street, and those on the side street closest to the centre of town, was ablaze with light in the same way as the mansion on the hill. Buildings of stone, brick and timber that were well built and carefully maintained – single and two storeyed commercial premises behind elevated sidewalks on the main street and houses in many styles fronted by yards along the residential streets to the south.

But there was no visible sign of life in the bright light of so many lamps that negated the glow of the moon in Elgin City. Nor any sound of it. Other than that of the man called Edge who rode his bay gelding by the limits marker and started along the centre of the broad street, sharply aware of being the object of mass attention but not sensing any threat hovering in the chill night air permeated with the smell of wood-smoke, simmering coffee and cooking food.

He rode between a barbershop and a blacksmith, a grocery store and the undertaking parlour of Samuel G. Gower, a feed and seed merchants run by a man named Gilmore and the Elgin City Bank, the First Class Restaurant and a stage line depot. Then ceased to scan the signs on the façades of the flanking buildings when activity and sound beyond the centre town intersection captured his low keyed attention – at about the same time as he realised that the brightly illuminated premises he rode between were temporarily deserted – and that maybe every citizen of Elgin was concentrated in the mid-town area. Where two men now appeared on the street, in front of two women who pressed the muzzles of revolvers into the napes of the men's necks.

The quartet appeared from behind a steepled church that faced the start of the side street, the women forcing the men at gunpoint to move awkwardly out to the centre of the intersection where, in tones too low for Edge to hear, the threatened pair were ordered to halt: and to turn toward the approaching rider.

The men's clumsy gait was enforced because they were tied together at the waist and chest and at the ankle, calf and knee of one leg: one man's left arm and the other's right was also lashed by ropes around

27

the shoulder of his fellow prisoner.

They were dressed like cowhands, but minus hats. About thirty years old, unshaven and dirty. Pale with fear and with the same emotion contorting their lean faces into masks of ugliness. The slightly shorter man whose right arm was not restricted by bonds had a gunbelt slung around his waist, but the holster was empty.

As soon as the terrified men were in the desired position – the revolvers still prodding the napes of their necks – people began to emerge from several nearby buildings. From the arched porchway of the church, from the meeting hall to the west of it, from the Delaware Saloon on one corner of the intersection and a few from the office of the Elgin County Herald on the opposite corner.

The vast majority of the people comprising the audience for what the tobacco chewing Sam Tufts had termed 'the show' made no attempt to conceal the reluctance with which they formed into two groups – out front of the church and across the start of the side street. Ordinary people, looking much like the citizens of any small frontier town where there was sufficient prosperity to be shared among all and the bad days were long gone and the future promised to be brighter even than the present.

But beneath the well fed, better than adequately clothed and robustly healthy outward appearance of the bulk of the population of this fine looking town there was shame and fear and humiliation and self reproach. Seen clearly on their faces as they shifted their gazes away from the helpless prisoners to look briefly – and overtly this time – at the lone rider moving along the street toward them.

These people – men and women of all ages from

28

about sixteen to perhaps ninety – had come out of the church and the meeting hall and the saloon. And were marshalled into the twin groups by the handful of people who emerged from the newspaper office. Six men – among them Gabe Millard and Bob Lowell – and three women. The stylishly attired gunslinger without a gunbelt very noticeable among the other men who were cast from the same mould as Hite and Tufts. And in their company the young Lowell looked tough and mean despite his round face and button eyes.

Likewise the women who wore six pointed stars of highly polished metal pinned to the left pockets of their shirts: as did the two escorts for the prisoners, Edge saw, when they moved away from the roped together men. Shirts were not the only masculine clothing the women wore, for the rest of their garb consisted of spurred boots, denim pants, kerchiefs and Stetsons. And all five of the female peace officers had gunbelts slung around their waists. Four of them with the butt of a revolver jutting from a tied down holster.

It was the oldest of the law women – by at least twenty years – who was missing a handgun. For it was one of the Army Model Colts that had urged the prisoners out to the centre of the street which she had dropped into the man's empty holster before moving away to play her part in the crowd control.

There was very little talk while the bizarre situation developed in the brightly lit mid-town area of Elgin City. And it was obvious that the local citizens were familiar with such events – needed simply to be encouraged to take their places rather than instructed by the hard men and the women with badges.

Only to the impassive Edge and to the trembling with dread, roped together prisoners was this whole experience with evil anything new.

Then a door was swung open and what slight mumbling of talk there had been was abruptly curtailed. At the same moment as Edge reined in the gelding and turned his head to look to his right. And see a man step over the threshold of a millinery store called Hedda's Hats, and greet effusively:

'It's Captain Josiah Hedges! There's no doubt about it, is there? The guy that rid the world of that murdering sonofabitch Elliot Thombs! I'm right ain't I, joe?'

'Just called Edge now, feller,' the half breed answered evenly as all attention reverted to him again.

'And I'm Mayor Earl Gray. Real anxious to get acquainted with you. Just as soon as I've attended to a little unfinished business.'

Edge shifted his unblinking gaze from Gray to the fear filled, roped together men on the centre of the street between the two groups of unwilling witnesses and growled: 'Plain to see those fellers are bound to be dealt with first.'

Four

EARL Gray was the big man of Elgin County in more than one sense of the term, for he was grossly, grotesquely fat. Was about five and a half feet tall but surely weighed in the region of three hundred and fifty pounds – and looked as if not a single ounce of this enormous bulk was comprised of firm flesh. He was almost as wide as the doorway of the hat store from which he emerged, and the boarding of the sidewalk groaned with strain as he angled across it and stepped down on to the dusty surface of the street. He was only sixty-five or so, but obesity caused him to move like a man a great deal older than this – he needed to grip a sidewalk roof support to steady himself as he moved from one level to another.

His shoulders were of the same width as his hips and there was no indentation at his waist. His belly and breasts bulged excessively and his rump also accommodated more than an equitable share of the man's blubber – so that these areas of his anatomy tremored and bounced in a jelly-like fashion as he moved. The animated bulges and the less pronounced flabbiness of his torso and limbs contoured by a yellow silk shirt with white fringes and black pants that may also have been of silk – were certainly of a sheened fabric.

His hat was a white Stetson with a tooled leather band and no sweat stains. Silver hair showed below its brim and he also had a straight moustache of thick growing silver hair. His face under the white brim of the hat and between the long sideburns of silver hair was stained dark brown by the elements and was engraved with myriad lines which were not deep because his skin was stretched taut by the thick layer of flesh that caused not one plane of his features to be angular. There was something about his rounded face with the wide apart dark eyes, broad mouth and slightly cleft chin that suggested he would have been handsome in the classical manner if he were not so obese. But his fatness of face did not make him ugly above the series of double chins that stepped down from his jaw to his chest. Rather, the bloated features gave him a look of avuncular geniality, even when he was not displaying his very white teeth in a happy smile – an expression which Earl Gray dropped the instant he shifted his eager gaze away from Edge to direct a fixed stare toward the hapless prisoners on the intersection. And moved carefully down off the sidewalk to waddle toward the terrified men, each of his pudgy, many ringed hands draped over the ivory gripped butts of matching Tranters in the decorative holsters hung from his silver buckled gunbelt.

The bite of night had a firm hold in the air now, but the roped together men were oozing sweat from every pore on their bristled, dirt grimed faces. And Gray sweated, too, but the moisture that Edge could see staining the back of the fat man's shirt was erupted by excitement rather than fear – an emotion

32

that was clear to hear in his voice when he came within forty feet of the men, halted, dropped his hands away from the revolvers and spoke into the silence which seemed to have a palpable presence in the chill, smoke smelling air pervading Elgin City.

'Okay, Magee. Figure I can plug you and Colly dead centre from this range. But I guess a thief like you isn't in that class. So you get the chance you were promised by my girl. You told them both how we handle this kind of thing hereabouts, Pearl?'

'Don't I always, Dad?' the oldest woman with a star answered – the one who had given her gun to Magee. And, as she responded to Gray, looked away for the first time from Edge who continued to sit his stationary gelding some thirty feet in back of where her father stood. Then she returned her gaze to the half breed, wearing the same expression of blatant appraisal as previously.

'Mr Gray – ' the prisoner without a gun pleaded as tears began to run with the sweat beads across his quivering cheeks.

'Mayor Gray, runt!' the fat man snarled viciously. 'I'm the mayor of this town and I own the whole frigging county around it! So you better act respectful or I'll see to it you die the hard way, Colly! With a slug in the gut and a lot of time to find out what that feels like!'

'I'm sorry, mayor!' the dread filled prisoner blurted. 'But we weren't stealin'! Not like we meant to steal! Magee and me didn't know we was on private range when we – '

'I thought you said you told them, Pearl,' Gray said in a groaning tone.

'I told them, Dad,' the fat man's daughter answered. 'And the girls was around when I did.

33

Ain't that right?'

The four younger women with stars on their shirts were all between twenty and twenty-five and as Pearl looked expectantly at each of them in turn, so did Edge. And he saw that they were all green eyed redheads – the same combination as the older woman – and that there were also other similarities shared by the group, in the make up of their features but not their builds. So guessed that Pearl was the mother and Gray was the grandfather of the four young law women who now all nodded emphatically to agree with what had been said. Excitedly eager for the killing to take place, while Pearl began to study Edge again, Gray sought to curb his anger, the hard men remained resentfully impatient and the reluctant audience expressed varying degrees of revulsion for the evil being enacted before it.

Everyone's expression clear to see in the bright lamp light that illuminated the main street from every window.

There were less people present on the occasion he killed Elliot Thombs in the state of Kansas back in 1865. And the midsummer night was lit only by the flames of a fire on which he was cooking supper while he dried himself after an invigorating swim in the Smoky Hill River.

His name had been Josiah C. Hedges when he made that night camp, but he was no longer a captain of Union cavalry. For the war that had divided the nation was newly over, and he was riding on personal business. Along a violence trail that was destined to be the route he travelled for the rest of his life.

Not by choice.

When he left the battlegrounds of the east behind him after the peace signing at the Appomattox Court House it was his intention to return to the family farmstead in Iowa and pick up the pieces of the life he had left there at the start of the bitter war. But fate decreed another course for him and he arrived home to find the farm destroyed by fire and his crippled kid brother a mutilated corpse at the mercy of a flock of buzzards.

Jamie's was not the only body sprawled on the front yard and because the soldier back from the war knew the second victim, he was able to put names to the five men responsible for the carnage and destruction. And, using his war taught skills, he was able to pick up their trail and follow it.

Was a long way from meeting up again with the five vicious killers who had served in his troop for most of the war when he made the night camp on the bank of the Smoky Hill River. And offered to share his fire and meagre food with seven other former Union soldiers heading home after the fighting or in search of some place where the living would be better than it had been before.

He had not known their names, but one of the veterans had eventually recognised Joe Hedges as an officer – a class of men this embittered private hated on principle. And in a sudden kill or be killed situation, the man who was Elliot Thombs took a heavy calibre bullet from a Remington revolver in the head. Then, moments later, a Mexican in the group mispronounced the ex-captain's name and Josiah Carl Hedges became simply Edge . . .

The prisoner named Magee snarled: 'Cut it out for Christsake, Colly! Can't you see the whole friggin' family is nuts! And people who ain't got all their marbles ain't likely to listen to reason! Nor take account of you beggin' for mercy!'

The man without a gun had extended his free hand, palm upward and fingers splayed in a pleading gesture that was augmented by the expression on his tear run and sweat beaded face. While his mouth worked but no words were uttered and he looked on the verge of collapse.

'You're not going to rile me, runt,' Earl Gray countered, fully in control of himself again. Calm in voice and bearing as he started slowly forward. 'Whenever you're ready, remember. You're not going to rile me, just like your buddy's whining isn't going to get him or you off the hook. You trespassed in Elgin County and you allowed your horses to feed on my range. And when two Deputy County Sheriffs told you you'd have to pay a fine, you figured to humiliate them because they're women.'

Earl Gray moved in his waddling walk at a pace that suggested he was wading through chest high water – with his thick arms arced out to the sides like he was using the bejewelled hands to steady himself. His corpulent flesh moved against the restraint of his sheened clothing, but his slightly curved hands were rock steady where they hovered on a level with the ornately butted Tranters in the decorative holsters. And his head was also immobile as he stared fixedly at Magee.

'We thought they was kiddin'!' Colly managed to squeeze out harshly around the near choking ball of fear in his throat. 'A couple of fine lookin' women like –'

'Fine looking women isn't what you called Laura and Joy, runt,' Gray interrupted as he continued to slowly and relentlessly narrow the gap on the roped together men.

Colly wrenched his head from left to right and back again; and then directed his pleading gaze above and beyond the obese man to meet the glint eyed impassiveness of Edge. Cried:

'We're strangers around here! What would any of you men do if you didn't know the set up? And a couple of young girls with tin stars say you gotta pay ten bucks apiece for grazin' your horse . . .'

Nothing in the face of anyone he saw offered him a trace of hope: and expanding terror totally choked off the words when his attention was drawn again to the bloated face of Earl Gray. Who allowed a second of silence to hang in the tension filled night before he continued as if there had been no interruption:

'Piece of ass is what you called Laura and Joy. And you offered to pay the fines in kind. Reckon it was quite a jolt to you two when those girls got the drop on you and run you into town easy as if you were a couple of day old critters wandered off from the herd.'

He had closed to within twenty feet of Magee and Colly now, his hands and head still not having moved even a fraction of an inch.

Colly now squeezed his eyes tightly closed and worked his lips rapidly but not emphatically as he prayed for divine intervention.

While Magee wore a scowl of hatred that narrowed his eyes, flared his nostrils and raised one side of his upper lip to expose a few tobacco discoloured teeth.

'But you two have to have something more coming to you than a jolt. Unless you're faster than me, Magee?'

'Just keep on comin', you barrel of lard, and you'll find out!' the man with the Colt in his holster countered.

'I'll keep on coming until you go for the gun, runt. And then I'll do my level best to kill you. For insulting two of my girl's girls. In a fair gunfight.'

'Fair my ass!' Magee rasped through the open part of his mouth.

Just fifteen feet separated Gray from the two prisoners now.

'It certainly is,' the fat man answered evenly. 'I'm a big target. Not because of any fault of mine. Have what's called a glandular defect, which is why I hate for people to needle me about my size. Not as if I overeat like lots of fat men.'

Magee began to bring up his right hand while he stared fixedly at the fleshy face of Gray.

'But me being such a big target, I figure it only right that it's the same *vice versa*. Pearl told you all this, but I guess you were too scared to listen.'

'We heard, you fat bastard,' Magee rasped. 'And Colly and me flipped a dime for the gun. On account of we're just cowhands, not gunfighters. And it don't make much of a difference seein' as how you got two irons and –'

Now Magee looked to either side of the street and along it – even over his shoulder. Anywhere but at Earl Gray and perhaps seeing nothing and nobody clearly. The scowl still firmly set on his darkly bristled features as he talked for the sake of it – giving the impression he was vainly seeking sympathy from the unresponsive watchers, while in fact he was obviously trying to lull the fat man into becomig distracted.

'That's because there's just me against the two of

you, runt.'

Magee's elbow bent enough for his hand to be level with the butt of the Colt. This at the instant his scowling gaze returned to the face of Gray. And he blinked and expressed dread of death as his curved fingers fisted around the butt of the woman's revolver: knowing with greater certainty than anything else he had ever known before that he was doomed.

The Colt came halfway out of the holster and his thumb cocked the hammer. But by then – the move so fast it was seen only in a blur – both the Tranters were clear of the fat man's holsters and were cocked and levelled.

Some of the reluctant watchers gasped, a few squealed and many averted their eyes. While the law women and the hard men stared fixedly with bright eyed wonder or malicious jealousy at the double killing staged in front of them. And a woman just inside the doorway of Hedda's Hats said dejectedly to the only person within earshot:

'What a shit he is.'

To which Edge, who had been aware of her on the threshold of the store for fully two minutes growled: 'You said it, lady.'

This spoken against the dual crack of the simultaneously fired Tranters, aimed from the broad hips of the fat man to explode the bullets on marginally differing trajectories. The revolver in his right hand triggering a shot to drill a hole in the chest of the praying Colly. While that in his left spat a maiming shell into the inner angle of Magee's right elbow – and out through the back. The impact swinging the arm to the rear as the shocked nervous system sprang open the man's hand so that the unfired Colt was pitched forward and down.

Earl Gray had halted for the part of a second it took to draw and fire the two guns. Now started forward again at the same slow pace as before, thumbing back both hammers without haste while smoke wisped from their muzzles. This as Colly died on his feet and started to fall backwards, his chin sunk to his chest like he was staring down in deep shock at the rapidly expanding stain of blood on his shirt front. And Magee, his face a grimacing mask of pain and dismay, ignored the limply hanging, bullet shattered arm to splay his legs and struggle manfully to remain erect. His teeth gritted between curled back lips, his eyes squeezed tightly closed, the veins in his neck standing out and his every pore squeezing sweat beads: while the dead weight of the man roped to him threatened to drag him down on to his back in the path of the advancing Gray.

His deep, desperate breathing was the only sound that reached the ears of the watchers as Magee's chest rose and fell in the same cadence as the relentless strides of his tormentor. Until one of the watchers heard another murmur:

'I ain't no lady, Joe. If I was, I wouldn't let myself be screwed by that shit.'

Gray came to a halt three feet away from Magee and bridged the distance by raising and extending his arms. Until the muzzles of the Tranters rested against the shoulders of the straining man. Who opened his eyes in response to the double pressures, brought his lips together and shaped them to spit into the obese face between the revolvers. But Gray squeezed the triggers a second time – in perfect unison again. And Magee vented a roar that owed as much to a sense of defeat as to pain as he was sent sprawling backwards: blood spurting from the entry wounds and spraying from the larger holes where the bullets exited.

There was a more vociferous reaction from the main body of unwilling watchers now, but snarling rebukes from the hard men and the daughter and granddaughters of Earl Gray brought back a grudging silence. In time for two more shots to sound as one in isolation – both aimed to drill bullets into the crotch of the broken Magee, drawing a high pitched scream of agony from deep inside him as more blood weltered to be soaked up by the arid street surface.

'Who's a man nobody would call gentle, like you see,' the woman in the store added dully in the wake of the scream: after Magee's back, arched by pain, collapsed and the man was inert and silent.

Perhaps dead, but Gray made certain of this with two more shots: the bullets exploded with the guns held at arms length, muzzles just three feet from the unfeeling head the bullets entered and left. Went in via both eyes and came out through the top rear of his skull.

Edge looked away from the grossly overweight man who remained standing over his victims – as unmoving as they were for stretched seconds – to gaze directly at the woman for the first time. And saw that she was a thirty year old black haired beauty with flawless skin and a slender build. And he growled as he dug in the shirt pocket for the makings:

'Can see why he has a crush on you . . .

She made a face like she was about to throw up, then reached to the side, grabbed the door and slammed it closed. And Edge completed:

'Since he ain't no gentleman and they're the ones take their weight on their elbows.'

41

Five

THE crowd began to disperse without the law women and the hard men needing to tell them. A
handful back into the church, some returning to the
saloon but most heading for the brightly lit stores
and other commercial premises or toward the houses
on the curving side street and its spurs.

The black clad Gabe Millard and the gunmen who
carried guns all went back into the corner office of
the Elgin County Herald. And the four younger
women with stars on their shirts headed for a place
beyond the church – from which one of them and
their mother had brought the condemned prisoners.

Edge swung down from the saddle then, having
rolled the cigarette while most of the Elgin City
people went back to whatever had occupied them
before the execution was signalled. Now struck a
match on his Winchester stock to light the smoke
and began to lead the gelding by the bridle toward
the intersection. Where Earl Gray holstered his
matching Tranters, his daughter came to stoop and
retrieve her unfired Colt and a short, stockily built
man of about forty with freckles covering his face
and bald head asked:

'Okay to haul away the cadavers, Mayor?'

'When there's trash on our streets, Sam, you know I like to have it cleaned up real fast,' the fat man replied to the only member of the enforced watchers who remained close to the scene of the double killing.

'I'll get right to it, sir,' the town undertaker assured and hurried along the western length of the main street toward his parlour that was almost at the end of it.

This as Edge reached the intersection and was able to see that the building set back between the church and a bakery was the law office and gaol – standing behind a cement apron on which stood a gallows.

'So you're the guy that killed Elliot Thombs?' Pearl said, peering hard at the half breed from close quarters for the first time. And then she nodded as he halted to submit to her study, meeting her appraising gaze with an impassive coldness in his slitted eyes. 'Yeah, I can see you ain't changed all that much from when the picture was done of you. Not really.'

The woman's red hair had a few strands of grey in it and the skin that was stretched taut over the fine bone structure of her face was extensively wrinkled in the areas of the eyes and the mouth. She looked to be about forty-five and unless her shape owed something to her undergarments she had taken as good care of her body as of her face. She was probably no taller than five feet three inches without the high heeled boots and the Stetson.

'My girl, Pearl Irish, Joe,' Earl Gray introduced, swinging clumsily away from the corpses as he dry washed his hands so that the precious metals of the rings clinked and the jewels of the settings sparkled in the bright light. While the smile that lit his heavily

43

fleshed features made it obvious he did not need this symbolic gesture to aid him in forgetting the evil he had just committed. 'Reason she has a different name to me, she was married one time. Had that string of girls that are her deputies – Joy, Laura, Anne and Gloria. Was widowed in the war. Guess there's no chance you ever ran across Captain Zach Irish? Was an infantry officer with Ambrose Burnside's Ninth Corps?'

'It was a big war,' Edge answered, aware that Pearl Irish was becoming impatient with her father.

'Mayor Gray or just mayor, Joe. Or sir if you like.'

The woman made a sound of mild disgust.

'It was a big war, mayor.'

'I make exceptions, some folks get to being ornery jealous, Joe. So I don't make exceptions.' He directed a withering look at his daughter.

'That apply to the five bucks it cost me to cross your property, mayor?'

'Chichenfeed, Joe!' Pearl answered before her father could respond. 'You're gonna be rich for what you done all that time ago to the skunk that –'

'Go attend to your duty, girl!' Gray cut in. 'Out here in the middle of the street isn't the right place to discuss business for a man of my standing!'

His tone of voice was not harsh, but there was a commanding glint in his dark eyes that his daughter knew better than to disobey.'

And she complained without force: 'But I oughta be around when you and Joe –'

'Going to have supper first, girl.' He took from a pocket of his silk shirt a gold watch and flipped open the lid. 'Shall we say in two hours – that'll be at nine thirty – at the house?'

He looked enquiringly at Pearl and at Edge. The woman nodded and explained:

'Dad means at the Triple X. You rode by it on the way to town.'

'I saw it, ma'am,' Edge answered around the cigarette as Pearl Irish turned to go toward the building in back of the gallows and Earl Gray waddled back the way he had come, heading for the millinery store. 'Planned on stopping over in town tonight, so I'll be able to make it.'

'You bet your ass you'll make it, Joe,' Gabe Millard called flatly from where he stood on the threshold of the newspaper office, a shoulder leaning on the frame.

And only the half breed looked at the black clad man. Neither the woman sheriff of Elgin County nor its owner and mayor reacted at all to the gunslinger's comment.

Gray said to Sam Gower as the freckle faced mortician led a horse along the street: 'Don't forget to pick up the paperwork from Mrs Irish and have Doc Hargrove issue death certificates, Sam.'

'Yes sir, mayor,' the man answered as Edge started forward with his horse again, bypassing the corpses Gower had come to collect and heading now along the eastern stretch of the brightly lit main street. Aware again of being covertly watched by many pairs of eyes and this time sensing resentment toward him.

Nobody looked at the half breed, though, when he raked his glinting eyed gaze from side to side – glancing through the screen of drifting smoke from the cigarette into the windows of the lamplit buildings. In the law office Pearl Irish was hunched in a chair behind a desk: writing while her daughters were grouped behind her, as intent as their mother on the paperwork. And across the street, Gabe Millard had closed the door of the newspaper office and gone to join another of the hired men beside a table where the young Bob Lowell and three others were playing a card game. There was a man and a woman in the bakery next to the law office and just a woman in the candy store next to the office of the Elgin County Herald. A lone man in the tailor's shop and another in the building with a sign that proclaimed it housed Doctor Horace J. Hargrove's Surgery and Dentistry.

But these and the occupants of other flanking buildings he passed on his way to the livery stable were all pointedly too busy to bother with what was happening out on the street while the newcomer to town surveyed them.

The liveryman, though, could not ignore the half breed who led the bay gelding into the stove heated, animal smelling stable: through a part open door which spilled its share of lamplight out into the chill night. Then the leather aproned, sixty year old, short but powerfully built man with an arc of grey hair around the sides and back of his head and wearing thick lensed eyeglasses had to interrupt his chore and acknowledge the existence of Edge.

'Gray kill people who talk to strangers without his permission, feller?' he asked as he halted the gelding and turned to close the door through which a stream of cold air was flowing.

'Don't do that, mister!' the liveryman called from the rear, rising suddenly from a bench beside the stove where he was soaping a saddle. His frown as anxious as his tone of voice. And he added plaintively: 'Please?'

'Your place,' Edge answered with a shrug, leaving the door open and scanning the stalls to either side of the building that was twice as deep as it was wide and contained two dozen stalls, only six of which were vacant.

'The mayor, he likes Elgin City to be bright when he comes to town, mister. And we all have to do our bit. This place not havin' no windows, I have to –'

'Your place, like I said,' Edge cut in on the man with bad eyesight who now spoke in an apologetic tone. 'I see you have the space to take care of my horse?'

'For just the one night, mister?'

'Reckon so.'

'Just board and feed?'

'And curry,' Edge said, running a hand over the neck of the gelding, the coat matted to the touch by the dried mud of trail dust mixed with sweat lather.

'Be five dollars, mister,' the liveryman said with a gulp. And blinked several times in quick succession behind the magnifying lenses of his spectacles when Edge froze in the act of unbuckling the saddle cinch.

'I said for just the one night.' He straightened, took the cigarette butt from his mouth, dropped it to the scrupulously clean hard packed dirt floor and crushed it beneath a boot heel.

The man at the bench nodded several times now, an expression of misery on his face and answered in a matching tone: 'I know, mister. But I gotta make a livin', too.'

Edge pointedly surveyed the eighteen occupied stalls as he growled: 'You aiming to get as rich as Gray, feller?'

'The mayor's got a four-fifths share in all Elgin City businesses, mister. He fixes the prices people

47

have to charge.'

Edge sighed and nodded. Took hold of the bridle again and told the liveryman: 'Too steep for me, feller.'

'Where you goin' with that horse?'

'Me and him bedded down in the open on a lot colder nights than this up in the mountains,' Edge told the again anxious man.

'That ain't allowed inside city limits, mister. Mrs Irish or one of her deputies'll haul you in for vagrancy.'

'There's a lot of open country outside of town.'

The liveryman shook his head. 'You seen what happened to them two cowhand drifters that allowed their horses to crop Elgin County grass, mister.'

'I paid the five dollars to –'

'Keep you from havin' to swing wide to get where you're headed, Joe,' Millard put in from the part open doorway. 'You have to pay for anythin' else you have in Elgin County.'

Pearl Irish, wearing a sheepskin coat similiar to the one Edge wore, stepped into view alongside the sardonically smiling black garbed gunman without a gun and said: 'There's been a change of schedule, Joe. Dad's on his way back to the Triple X now and we have to get right after him.'

'Fine,' the half breed said and made to turn the gelding all the way around so he could lead him outside.

'Leave your horse with Devine, Joe,' Millard said. 'I'll drive the two of you and bring you back.'

'And pick up the tab here, feller?'

'I told you, Joe!' the woman said impatiently. 'Dad's gonna make you a rich man. In a little while, five dollars to you is gonna be no more than a drop in the ocean.'

'See?' Gabe Millard growled.

'Sure,' the half breed answered. And surrendered his horse to Devine who had come from the rear to the front of his livery.

The woman turned and moved away from the stable entrance as Millard rasped through teeth that were now exposed in a scowl instead of the sardonic smile:

'So best you don't make waves, mister?'

He backed off the threshold to allow Edge to step across it.

'Or I could be all washed up?'

It was not so bright outside now and the level of light continued to fall as the businesses and professional people of Elgin City doused their lamps, locked up their premises and headed for home along the street that curved south between the two hills. This as a canopy top country wagon with a single horse in the traces rolled out of town on the west trail, its black and gold paintwork gleaming in the moonlight that was now predominant in the night.

'Gray afraid of the dark, feller?' Edge asked as Devine closed the livery door and Millard started to follow Pearl Irish – across the front of Reece's Wagon Hire which was next to the stable and into the alley on the far side of it.

'My Dad ain't afraid of a damn thing, Joe!' the woman snapped. 'And you better talk respectful about him even when he can't hear you. I'll go along with *Mister* Gray.'

The two storey building housing the wagon hire business was already in darkness and just a little moonlight found entrance to the alley, to show that a rockaway with a two horse team was parked there.

With a fat man – but nowhere near as fat as Earl Gray – holding the bridle of one of the animals.

'Things sure happen fast and sometimes without fuss around here,' Edge said as the woman swung open a door and climbed into the carriage. And Gabe Millard heaved himself up into the three way protected driver's seat – neither he nor the man holding the horse having offered Pearl Irish any help.

'Have time to go home for my supper before you folks get back, Mr Millard?' the fat man asked humbly.

'Depends how fast you eat and how long we are, Wiley,' Millard told him as Edge got aboard and closed the door. Then was driven hard on to the seat beside the woman by the suddenness of the rock-away's start.

'Fast service without no fuss is somethin' of what you get for the high prices you gotta pay in Elgin, Joe,' Pearl Irish said dully as the carriage made a turn to the west out of the alley. 'Dad wants the best of everythin' and expects the folks that live here to give it. And get it, same as he does. Reason nothin's cheap hereabouts.'

In the confines of the passenger section of the rockaway the Elgin County sheriff even smelled like a man – wore no powders or paints or perfumes.

'Except life, ma'am.'

'We gotta have rules. And if you got rules you gotta punish people that breaks them.'

The rockaway rolled by the premises of Doctor Hargrove which was one of the few buildings on the main street which was still lit. The tall and thin, pale complexioned medical man was on the threshold of his surgery, along with Sam Gower whose horse with

50

the corpses slung over its back was hitched to a sidewalk roof support nearby. The two men watched with obvious distaste as the carriage was driven by.

Edge said: 'I didn't see any sign that warned people to keep off the grass.'

'Not knowin' the law ain't no excuse for breakin' it Joe!' Pearl Irish intoned, as if it was a line she had learned by rote and used often. 'And it wasn't for lettin' their horses steal Dad's grass them two cowpunchers had to go up against him. It was for what they was tryin' on with my two girls. If their Dad had been alive, he'd have defended the girls' honour. Way things are, their Granddaddy had to do it. If them two cowpunchers had just done like they was told by Laura and Joy, all it would've cost them was a five dollar fixed penalty, Joe. Ten in all, that right?'

'Fine.'

Six

THE newspaper office on one corner of the side street was still ablaze with light and across from this in two directions, the law office behind the gallows and the Delaware Saloon were also lit: but in a more subdued way.

Just two of Pearl Irish's daughters could be seen in the law office and there was no longer anybody watching the four handed card game in the building housing the Elgin County Herald. Business was slow in the saloon and the handful of patrons visible from the rockaway looked not to be enjoying themselves when they glanced up from their drinks at the sound of the carriage on the street.

'Fred Garner that has the saloon is a real expert on Indians, Joe,' the woman said suddenly, as the rig rolled along the western stretch of the main street that was deserted and lit only by the moon.

'He is?'

'Seems Wyomin' is a little bit of a Delaware Indian word. Means somethin' about on the big plain, There's a place in the state of Pennsylvania called Wyomin' Valley where the Delaware Indians used to be. Did you know that, Joe?'

'No, ma'am, I didn't know that.'

'And I guess you don't care too much?'

'No, ma'am, not too much.'

'Me neither, not really. Just that Fred Garner and me, we used to walk out and if we'd got married, it'd been better if we had somethin' in common.'

Edge said nothing in response to the woman who he guessed was simply talking for the sake of it – perhaps because she was uncomfortable with silence between them or maybe as an outlet for the frustration of loneliness.

'You ever get married, Joe?'

'Yes, ma'am. She died.'

'Like my Zach.'

The rockaway was off the street now, beyond the city marker and on the trail at the base of the hill with the Triple X ranch house on its crest. Many light sources glittered through the foliage of the pinyons that partly obscured the house on this side.

Edge met and married Beth Day a long time after the killing of Elliot Thombs that made him a wanted man with an assumed name. And they settled down on a farmstead in the Dakotas at the end of a trail that had run for countless miles in every direction across a landscape over which violence constantly hovered – and often swooped to strike. During a time when the man who had become Edge was forced to acknowledge that the sole reason for him living was life itself. Which he could preserve only by using the harshly learned lessons of the war and by remaining the dehumanised being behind the gun that war had made him.

This was his fate, he had convinced himself: until Beth Day entered his life. And he knew that this woman could not be placed in the same category as the pleasures, luxuries and sometimes the essentials that he had to take, make use of and pay for as and when they came within his reach. So he attempted to cheat his fate. To return to working the soil on a place that was much more on a scale with the Hedges family farmstead in Iowa than this rich spread in Wyoming.

But the Sioux came, and Beth suffered a horrifying death in a manner that forced her husband to accept the blame.

That terrible time was long gone now. A time of searching and finding and killing. And of the contemplation of suicide, he was lately able to admit to himself – for years he had refused to acknowledge that he'd considered such a sure way to end what he endured in the wake of Beth's dying: while he was in a drunken stupor and prey to insidious attacks of self-pity. But he beat the fate that beckoned him so alluringly toward defeat. And rode out again on to the dangerous land where the threat of death was always as close to him as was his shadow in midday sunlight: and where he was now more competent than ever to survive against the odds. Because he was convinced by the tragic experience of the death of his wife, he was destined never to have and to hold for long anything that was worthwhile – outside of his own continued existence.

And so it was without the hopes and dreams of any ambition beyond the simple one of staying alive that he had ridden the endless and aimless trail that brought him to Elgin County. A man with few needs and no wants, without pretensions or pretence – except toward himself at first when he would not admit that he had sunk so deep into a slough of depression, fate had almost won.

Gabe Millard swung open the right side of the rockaway and growled with bad grace: 'Here we are, Mrs Irish.'

His announcement cut across whatever the woman was talking about to swamp the silence and interrupted the half breed's train of absorbing thought. And both passengers were mildly surprised to realise the carriage was halted at the foot of the broad steps which led up to the terrace out front of the brightly lit house.

Pearl Irish climbed eagerly out on to the gravel surfaced driveway, a strained look on her heavily wrinkled and unmade-up face as if the effort to talk silence out of existence during the short trip from town had drained her emotional reserves. While the half breed stepped down from the rockaway with his features impassive and no feeling of self disgust for being so withdrawn that he had failed to be aware of what was happening around him for long minutes. For the line of his thinking had a bearing on his present circumstances and he had trusted his sixth sense for impending danger to signal a warning if a threat appeared.

'Nice smooth ride, feller,' Edge said to Millard, who had not helped the woman from the rockaway: instead had started to go toward the country wagon with the canopy top that was parked in front of the larger rig. 'But I don't tip.'

'Let me give you one, mister!' the gunman without a gun rasped as the red headed Bob Lowell leaned over the side of the country wagon's driver's seat at the sound of the harshly spoken words. 'You ain't as good as you think you are.'

'And it sounds like you ain't as modest as you said you were, feller,' Edge answered as he followed the woman up the steps.

'Sometimes the kid here ain't on the ball, Joe.'

'After Mayor Gray, Gabe's the best there is, stranger!' Bob Lowell said enthusiastically.

'First is first, second is nowhere,' Earl Gray announced flatly from the top of the steps. And directed a complacent smile down at the abruptly self conscious Lowell and the again self controlled Millard. Then injected surface warmth into the expression as he spread his thick arms to the sides and turned to usher Edge and his daughter toward the house. 'Come along in, Joe. And kindly forgive the change in our arrangement. Which was intentional from the outset.'

As the newcomers went by him, he moved between them with his arms down at his sides again. But his voice retained the effusive tone when he continued as they crossed the flagged terrace:

'A man does not become as successful as I have without the assistance of high quality help, Joe. Nor stay at the top. And to make sure his help stays high quality, he has to keep them on their toes. One way of doin' that is to spring changes on the bastards. Surprise them and check they keep pace with the changes you make.'

They had entered the house through a double doorway and Pearl held back to close the studded oak doors. Edge glanced over his shoulder at her and was in time to glimpse the embittered grimace she directed at her obese father before she turned. And the fat man gestured with a pudgy hand for the half breed to enter an arched doorway into a room on the left. Waddled ahead of his guest from the chandelier lit, wood panel walled, highly polished floored, night air cooled hallway into a sitting room. Which was as spacious and elegantly furnished and decorated as the hall. But was warmed by a blazing log fire in an ingle fireplace and had a deep pile carpet on the floor. And the walls were stucco, hung with a score of paintings in gilt frames.

The black haired beauty with the perfect complexion from the millinery store sat on a sofa set at right angles to one side of the fireplace. She was dressed in the same plain black dress that fitted snugly to her slender figure as when he first saw her. Just as the fat man had not changed from the white fringed yellow shirt and sheened black pants – but he no longer wore the gunbelt with the matching Tranters, or the white Stetson.

Edge removed his hat and nodded a greeting to the woman who smiled with what seemed to be genuine warmth. But could not have been because she shared the expression between the two men, one of whom she had called a shit and the other she had so obviously disliked on first meeting.

'This is Hedda Trask, Joe,' Gray introduced as he lowered himself carefully on to the centre of an identical sofa across the front of the fireplace from the woman. 'Hedda and me have an understandin'. That's fine there, Joe.'

Edge had advanced halfway into the room and came to a halt as the fat man spoke the instruction and Pearl Irish stepped across the threshold and closed the door. Which placed him midway between the blazing fire and the window that spilled light out across the terrace. Fifteen feet from each and also equidistant from Gray and Hedda Trask. Who he turned to face as the fat man's daughter angled across the room to join the millinery store owner, and immediately looked less feminine than ever in comparison with the beautiful woman at her side.

'My girl is family so has the run of the house, Joe,' Gray said in the same even tone as before and with the smile still sitting easily on his bloated features. 'And the plan is that Hedda'll be family some day soon. You're just a passin' through stranger owed a favour. That I intend to repay. Nothin' else.'

There was a large, square mirror hung on the wall above the double decker mantelshelf in which the half breed was able to see a reflection of most of the room and of himself – standing hat in hand, unshaven and grimed with trail dust, dressed in the worse for wear outfit of shirt, pants, boots and sheepskin coat with the butt of the Frontier Colt jutting from the holster tied down to his thigh and causing the hem of the coat to be slightly rucked up.

Just for a part of a second did he glimpse the merest suggestion of high anger show in the glint of his ice blue eyes between the narrowed lids. Before he controlled the emotion within him and masked any outward clue to what he felt. And said:

'You don't owe me a thing.'

The fat man held up a hand and the jewelled rings on the stubby fingers glinted in competition with the half breed's eyes – but needed the light sources from the fire and the lamp chandelier to do this.

'Nobody argues with Earl Gray in his home, his town or his county, Joe.' The smile was gone now and the tone of voice was the same one he had used during the preamble to the double killing – after he controlled his rage. 'In the June of 'sixty-five, you met up with seven men just mustered out of the

Union army. One of them named Elliot Thombs was the bastard who murdered my son-in-law. Stuck Zach Irish with a knife after the Petersburg battles a couple of months earlier. Stuck him just because Zach give him an order he didn't like. Then the bastard ran – deserted just before the peace signin'. Not givin' a shit that my girl was left a widow with four girls of her own to raise.'

Gray turned his head to spit in the fire and while his face was averted, the two women briefly changed their expressions – which had been of melancholy reflection since the fat man had started to talk about the killing of Captain Zach Irish. Now, just for a second at the most and independently of each other, the widow expressed tacit bitterness toward her father and the woman he had plans to marry directed a scowl of deep seated hatred at him.

'I didn't do no fightin' in the war, Joe. Too busy out here in the West. Grubbin' for gold in California, learnin' the cattle ranchin' business in Texas and the south west territories and generally gettin' money to make more money. And learnin' how to protect what I worked friggin' hard for against the bastards that figured to take it off me easy. Man don't get to be fast as you saw I was any other way than by hard work. And for a man my size – on account of a glandular defect, Joe, not overeatin' – it's harder to do most things.'

Now he just shook his head and Hedda Trask almost made the mistake of scowling her hatred at him again when she thought he was going to take the time to spit in the fire.

'But I'm gettin' off the point, Joe.'

'I was gonna say that, Dad,'

Edge put his hat back on and rasped the back of a

hand over the bristles along his jawline, Then dropped the hand down at his side just behind the jutting butt of the Colt.

Gray directed one of his withering looks at his daughter and went on: 'Soon as I heard about Zach bein' murdered by one of his own men, I went lookin' for that man. Left behind every friggin' thing I'd worked my balls off for and went lookin'. Pretty soon found out Thombs was dead. Tracked down a Mexican he was ridin' with and he told me how it happened. And found out the Kansas law wanted you for murderin' the bastard. Nothin' I could do, seemed to me. So I come back out West with just one of the wanted posters that was issued for you in Kansas. And when I got back – had a place down in the south west territories then – I found a bunch of four CSA deserters had jumped my claim. And was a long way toward cleanin' out that motherfrigger of a lode.

'And I knew, Joe, that if I hadn't got back when I did – if I was chasin' the killer of Zach Irish all over the country – them bastards would have kept me from gettin' to be rich. And one of the things I liked best about bein' in this vale of tears, Joe, is bein' rich. Which is why I've had the word out to look for you ever since the lode them bastards located started to pay off. So you can share in my good fortune. How does one hundred thousand dollars sound to you, Joe?'

'Quite a number, feller.'

'Mayor, Mayor Gray or sir, Joe,' the grossly overweight man in the sheened, too snug fitting clothes said with a sigh and looked just mildly irritated at having had to remind the half breed again.

'Make you a deal,' Edge offered.

And Gray was too intrigued by the evenly spoken invitation to take exception to the lack of the courtesy title again. 'A deal?'

'You keep the hundred thousand bucks and I'll ride off your property tonight so I won't have to call you anything.'

Earl Gray sighed again and this time there was a degree of light in his widely spaced dark eyes that pointed to a more explosive sentiment than mild irritation.

'You already have the money, Joe,' he said, making an effort to remain self controlled which showed in the way his fleshy face became beaded with sweat. 'When Gabe and the Lowell kid came in from the Sweetwater crossin' and said they were almost sure it was you behind them, I had Joshua Morrow of the Elgin City Bank and Trust open an account in your name. And transfer the money from my account to the new one.

'There ain't a thing wrong with the money, Joe. It's all honestly earned in the line of business.'

'Not by me, feller. Put a bullet in the head of Elliot Thombs to keep him from killing me. If it happened to do you a favour –'

'You're arguin' with me in my home, Joe!' the fat man cut in, and his tone was shriller now. He took a handkerchief from a white frilled pocket of his shirt and patted the sweat off his brow and cheeks: and took the heat out of his voice to warn: 'Don't do it anymore. And call me what I insist on bein' called. Or all your new found wealth will buy is one hell of a rich man's funeral.'

Edge remained unblinkingly impassive and did not move a muscle in his tall, lean frame as Earl Gray delivered the ultimatum. And was aware of the switch to cool composure made by the fat man, the tacit plea for him to do what her father demanded on the timeworn face of Pearl Irish and the half smile of contempt that played on the lips of the beautiful Hedda Trask. This as his sixth sense for a lurking threat rang a warning at the forefront of his mind – after he had seen in the mirror an indistinct image of something moving just outside the window fifteen feet behind him.

'You're the wrong gender to be a mare, feller,' the half breed said flatly, his stance of apparent relaxed nonchalance unaltered. 'But you sure as hell are getting to be something of an old nag.'

Seven

EARL Gray's very white teeth gleamed between his drawn back lips as his fleshy cheeks and his many chins quivered and his bejewelled fingers clawed at the fabric covering of the sofa. Then his mouth gaped wide and he bellowed: 'Gabe!'

This as his daughter became crestfallen and the beautiful face of Hedda Trask continued to display contempt for Edge, but now the expression tempered with something that was close to pity.

The half breed remained tense like a wound spring behind the wafer thin shell of seeming unguardedness for the two seconds that separated his voice from that of the fat man's. Not trusting either of the women or the shaking Gray to be projecting the emotions they actually felt.

Just like him.

The door in the arch came forcefully open, burst inward with the crash of a booted foot kicking it. As Edge reached a decision about the two women and the man on the sofas – they were no immediate threat. And for just a part of a second his eyes, narrowed to the merest slivers of glittering blue, shifted the direction of their ice cold gaze to the mirror: specifically to the reflected image of the window behind him. Where, at the instant after the kick began to fold the door inward, he saw the eagerly smiling face of Bob Lowell – pressed so close to the pane that the kid's nose was flattened at the tip. Seen clearly, then partially obscured by the mist of condensation on the glass when Lowell breathed out.

Edge was already starting to rake his gaze away from the mirror by then – eyes racing along the sockets as he also turned his body, dropped into a crouch and brought his right hand into his side. The door hit the inner wall and his clawed hand fisted around the butt of the Frontier Colt. This at the moment that the face and form of Gabe Millard came into sharp focus. The gunslinger from Dodge City now without his frock coat and no longer minus the tools of his deadly trade – a .45 calibre Smith and Wesson Schofield with a wooden butt in a cutaway holster tied down to his left thigh, and a sawn off Purdy double barrel shotgun clutched in his right hand.

The shotgun was already angled to draw a bead on a target and the hammers were cocked as the black clad man stood splay legged on the threshold of the room, his pale face still seeming somehow mournful despite the grin he directed toward Edge. Then he squeezed the two triggers to explode the twin loads of shot with a deafening roar, a double flash and a billowing cloud of smoke.

At the same moment clawed the Smith and Wesson from the holster, thumbing back the hammer as part of the same series of smooth movements. In precisely the same manner as did Edge – but the half breed was fractionally faster: unprovoked by the discharging of the shotgun that had served to make Gabe Millard over confident. The Dodge City gunslinger obviously certain the sight and then the blast of the Purdy would distract Edge. But instead the half breed's moves were completed in a manner that took account of just one fundamental fact – his life was in danger from at least one source.

And he dealt with this first – drew, cocked, aimed and fired the Frontier Colt at the chest, left of centre, of the blond haired, pale faced man in black at the arched doorway. While he was starkly aware of the shotgun being fired, and knew he was not its target. The revolver in the rock steady left hand of Gabe Millard was the threat.

The gunslinger was not clearly seen at the moment Edge squeezed the trigger of the Colt: was distorted by the muzzle flashes and smoke of the Purdy's firing, and by the sudden move the half breed had to make – to hurl himself to the right, down at the floor and into a roll. To get out from under the six lamp chandelier that was torn out of the ceiling by the twin loads of the shotgun.

Pearl Irish and Hedda Trask screamed in unison and Earl Gray vented a bellow of rage that sounded like a giant wild animal in great pain. This against the crash and shatter of the chandelier hitting the carpeted floor and the lamps breaking to spray oil and flame in all directions. So that the low groan uttered by Gabe Millard was unheard by anybody but the man himself: as the sad grin froze on his face, he looked down at the bloodstain blossoming on the dark fabric of his shirt front and then died on his feet. The shotgun slipped from his right hand and the revolver from his left, his arms fell limply to his sides and his knees bent so that he fell forward into the room and lay prone and inert.

Edge powered into a final roll and brought up his

head and the freshly cocked Colt toward the window he was much nearer now. Saw Bob Lowell's face still pressed against the pane which was no longer fogged: because the kid was holding his breath in shock, excitement displaced by horror on his round, button eyed countenance.

'Water! Bring water! My house is burnin' down!'

Desperation drove Earl Gray's voice to a shrill pitch against the crackling of raging flames; before the black smoke hit the back of his throat and he began to cough and choke. And then footfalls sounded on the carpeted floor, running lightly. While Lowell dragged his stunned gaze away from the corpse of the man he had admired so much to locate the killer. Then executed a violent shake of his head that seemed to deny everything he had seen, before he drew back from the window, whirled and raced away across the flagged terrace.

Edge lunged up from the floor then, gaze and gun tracking across half the smoke filled, flame illuminated room. And saw Hedda Trask lift the skirt of her dress to step over the corpse of Gabe Millard and get out of the room. Close behind her, Pearl Irish had less difficulty negotiating the dead man because she wore pants. The obese Gray, a handkerchief pressed to his mouth, came to an abrupt halt in the wake of the fleeing women when the gun in the brown skinned hand of the half breed drew a bead on him.

Then he moved the mask against smoke and fumes to plead: 'Let me explain, Joe?' and his eyes glistened with tears of fear, grief, pain or lost hope.

'After this, feller, I don't figure we should be on speaking terms,' Edge told him harshly, through teeth clenched in the grin of a killer.

And the fat man thought his time was up – pressed

the handkerchief back to his mouth and vomited into it as he lunged out through the doorway, one booted foot stomping on an unfeeling arm of the corpse.

Edge followed him with less obvious haste – taking long strides to swing around the rapidly spreading flames. The revolver still in his hand until he emerged into the hallway. Where Gray leaned into an angle of two walls below the curve of the staircase, being wetly and malodorously sick to his stomach; while Hedda Trask looked at him with a strange mixture of revulsion and joy; Pearl Irish sat on a chair with her face in her hands, sobbing; and a half dozen Chinese servants of both sexes remained crowded in a doorway from the rear of the house, each holding a pail of water.

He holstered the gun then, and gestured with his head for the frightened Chinese to start fighting the fire as he stooped, took a grip on one of Gabe Millard's ankles and dragged him out into the hallway. Growled at the corpse: 'In our business, feller, first is first and second is dead, right?'

The Chinese went silently into the firelit room and then became excitedly noisy as they flung water at the flames and ran toward the rear of the house again to refill the pails.

Edge started down the centre of the brightly lit hallway toward the double entrance doors and the woman sheriff curtailed her sobs to ask plaintively:

'Where you goin', Joe?' Then snarled at the scurrying, chattering Chinese: 'Shut up, you foreign creeps!'

Her words alerted the fat man to the fact that the half breed was leaving and he struggled to quell his now dry retching as he straightened and turned from the corner, scrubbing at his vomit run chins with the handkerchief.

'To eat,' he answered with just a glance back as he eased open one of the doors with his left hand – the right poised to draw the Colt again should Lowell have recovered from his horror and be out on the terrace with lethal intent. But the terrace was deserted in the moonlight and that which spilled from the windows of the big house. There was a lot of moon shadow among the plantings to either side of the curving driveway, though, and Edge remained tense to respond to the first sign of aggression.

'You won't get outta my town alive unless – ' Gray started to rasp.

'Dad, that ain't no way to get what you want from a man like Joe. Not after you pulled that rotten trick on him. Let me try to tell him – '

The fat man started forward to catch up with the half breed who stepped out into the night, ignoring his daughter as she rose from the chair. Until she reached out with a hand to catch hold of his shoulder and restrain him. When he moved one of his hands with the same speed he had drawn against Magee and Colly causing the action to show as a mere blur. The back of it cracked sharply against the face of the woman and sent her staggering away from him with a scream of pain and shock – blood spurting from two ragged wounds gouged across her wrinkled cheek by jewelled rings when he brought his hand suddenly down before pulling it back.

'Not even family in my own friggin' house!' Gray roared as Pearl Irish was slammed hard down on to the chair. And Edge paused to look back into the house, as the fat man lowered his voice but kept the harsh tone to warn: 'You better believe me, Joe. You just go waltzin' into town alone, you'll be shot down like a mad dog. Just want some more talk is all. And if you wanna eat you can do it here at the house, for free.'

Steam had taken the place of smoke coming from the arched doorway to the sitting room and now this evaporated as the Chinese ceased their to-ing and fro-ing and disapeared into the rear of the mansion; anxious to be gone from the area which was pungent with the stink of doused burning and tense with the threat of renewed violence.

'It's the truth!' Pearl Irish blurted emphatically and shot a defiant look toward her father. 'Without Dad or me along with you, my girls and the men will –'

'I've got the message,' Edge cut in on her as he swung back across the threshold, and used a boot heel to close the door. 'What's for supper?'

Earl Gray grinned broadly and his daughter expressed relief: while standing in back of them, Hedda Trask stoked up some more scorn for the half breed.

'How do you like your steak, Joe?' the fat man asked.

'I'm real hungry, feller. Just cut off its horns and wipe its ass.'

Eight

THE fat man said, after the two Chinese women who served the meal had left the dining room: 'I'm gonna say somethin' to you now, Joe, that I ain't said in so long I maybe don't even recall how to pronounce it right. Just two words to start – I'm sorry.'

Just fifteen minutes had elapsed since Edge re-entered the house, convinced that the Gray father and daughter had told the truth. In that time, he had sat in the carver chair at one end of a long table which could accommodate twelve diners in the elegantly furnished room, again with an arched doorway, immediately across the hall from the fire damaged sitting room. While, on instructions from the fat man, Pearl Irish returned reluctantly to town to report to those who needed to know the events at the house and Hedda Trask went to the kitchen to supervise the cooking of the meal – without any unwillingness to be out of the presence of the two men she so despised. And Earl Gray himself climbed the stairway to go wash up and change from the vomit smelling clothes.

During the time he was alone in the dining room, Edge sipped good Kentucky bourbon at the invitation of the fat man and thought again briefly along the line that had occupied him on the ride out to the house in the rockaway. And smiled as he sat down at the rosewood table with its silver place settings – relishing the fine taste of the bourbon and appreciating the richness of his surroundings, but knowing that he would later be able to drink the cheapest Snakehead whiskey in the crudest of saloons with the same satisfaction and no rueful memories of his present circumstances.

He was just beginning to recall the last occasion when somebody had tried to give him a lot of money for, to his mind, no good reason, when Earl Gray entered the dining room with the salver-bearing Chinese girls at his heels. Just a tenth of the hundred thousand dollars this viciously evil, grossly obese man wanted to settle on him. His would-be benefactor then had been a woman, who when he refused to accept the cash had given him a half share in a saloon. Not the crudest in the west. Her name had been, like the glass he sipped this good bourbon from, Crystal . . .

Edge put the past out of mind as the fat man sat down in a matching carver chair at the far end of the elongated table: and snarled rasping imprecations for the servants to hurry. Gray did not mention Hedda Trask and why she was not with them for the meal, which was just a single course of steak and potato and salad – the portions for the larger man less than half the size of those given to the guest.

'Reckon if I had a house like this and I thought it was burning down, I'd feel pretty damn sick, feller,' Edge answered.

'I was sick with rage!' Gray shot back and paused to calm himself. 'At what that bastard Millard did. What I'm apologisin' for is puttin' you to the test the

71

way I did.' Edge had finished cutting meat and now used his fork to begin eating it: not taking his slitted eyes in the grimed and bristled face off the freshly washed up and changed – into a blue shirt with white fringes and unsheened black pants – fat man some fifteen feet away.

'You surprised me, feller. But I aim to stay on my toes by – '

'Joe, I'd like you to listen to me,' Gray cut in with a mixture of vehemence and pleading in his tone and on his face. 'And all I want you to say when I'm through is yes or no. Will you agree to do that?'

'If silence really was golden, I'd be able to afford the whole of Wyoming instead of just one county, feller.'

The fat man breathed in deeply and nodded as he set down his fork – like he did not want anything as distracting as eating to interfere with what he needed to say.

'Zach Irish wasn't simply my son-in-law, Joe. He was the best friend I ever had – maybe the only friend, I'm prepared to admit. And I was ready to spend the rest of my life huntin' for the bastard that killed him. But like you know, I didn't have to do that. And it's because I didn't have to do it that I got to be so rich. You made it that way and so it's natural, seems to me, that I feel I oughta reward you.'

'I told you no, feller.'

'I ain't through!' This was blurted out and the tone was immediately regretted. And he needed again to pause so that he could get his temper back under control before he continued: 'You're exceptional, Joe. Most everybody I've ever met wanted to be rich. And them that were rich already wanted to be richer. It's in the nature of most people, seems to me,'

He shook his head from side to side, frowning as if he was giving the intriguing puzzle a final few seconds of thought. But he failed to come up with the solution and now shrugged as if it no longer mattered. Went on:

'Gabe Millard was my top hand for more than two years, Joe. Came to town on the stage from Cheyenne because he'd heard I was always lookin' for good men of his kind to keep protected what I owned. Got from new man to top man in three days. By beatin' up on two guys and shootin' down another. With the fastest draw I ever seen – until today. And I'm includin' my own draw in that, Joe.'

He looked expectantly along the table to invite a comment from the half breed. But Edge simply chewed some steak, swallowed it and forked another piece into his mouth.

'I knew it, Joe. When Gabe and the Lowell kid rode into town from the Sweetwater crossin' and I was told it might well be you headin' for Elgin City, I knew you could handle Gabe. And the kid both, if he poked his nose in. I knew it from what I've heard about you, Joe. From all over and all sorts of people. On account of it's known far and wide I had an interest in you and so stories about you reach me every now and then . You'll be surprised how much I know about you, Joe?'

His tone and a slight elevation of his eyebrows added the query to make the statement a question. And on this occasion, Edge filled the pause. Said flatly:

'You surprise me again, feller, and the fat will really be in the fire. If you understand what the hell

I'm talking about?'

Earl Gray squeezed his dark eyes tightly closed and then massaged the lids with his ringed fists. Said while he was doing this: 'You can judge how highly I think of you, Joe, by the way I'm near bustin' a gut to be patient with you. The quickest way to blow my top is to pass remarks about my weight, which ain't my damn fault.'

He dropped his hands and opened his eyes, all traces of rage gone. Saw that Edge was calmly eating again, and nearing the end of the meal.

'I'll get to the point. From what I'd heard about you, on the top of what I owe you, I wanted you as the top man around here, Joe. And when I saw you, I wanted it double.

'Gabe had told me what I'd heard a dozen times already – that you ain't the kind that does anythin' you don't want to. Not to horse around, that you're an ornery sonofabitch. And, again not to horse around, I played on that part of you to set up the shoot out with Gabe. Took into account as well that Gabe made it pretty plain to me he didn't much like you.'

The fat man was talking fast now, obviously anxious to be finished with his explanation and proposition before Edge was through eating – as if he was afraid that his words alone would not be appealing enough to keep the half breed at the house.

'He didn't much like me either, Joe. Same as everybody who knows me. Because I ain't a very likeable person. The way I am and I won't ever change. And don't have to: because I want to be liked the way most everybody else wants to be hated – not at all. And I can afford to pay for everythin' I want, includin' what men with good buddies get for nothin'.

'Because most everybody has a price, Joe. And whatever it is, I can pay it. You know what I paid Gabe Millard? A grand a month is what I paid him. Top hand before him got two hundred a month. But Gabe said he felt naked without that S & W on his belt. For a thousand a month, though, he was ready to live with the feelin' of bein' naked – and wear his pistol only when I told him he could.

'See, Joe, I felt uncomfortable havin' Gabe around me with a gunbelt on when I knew he could outdraw me. And a man rich as I am didn't oughta be uncomfortable. Don't you agree?'

Gray had slowed the rate of talk as he digressed: and his intense expression faded to be replaced by a thoughtful frown. While the gaze from his wide apart eyes seemed to be fixed on an image of acute interest in the middle distance off to the right.

Edge chewed and swallowed a final piece of steak, rattled his fork down on the plate and asked: 'This where you want me to say yes or no, feller?'

The fat man jerked his mind's eye away from the reverie and was abruptly angry again – but at himself rather than with the half breed looking impassively along the table at him.

'Damnit, I ain't one usually to horse around, Joe. Just that so much has happened tonight, I guess. Look, I told Gabe to be ready to go up against you if I yelled for him, Joe. Knowin' deep down inside that you'd beat him to the draw. Wanted him dead, Joe. Because I wanted – want – you as the top hand around here. And there ain't no way that could be with Gabe Millard still around.

'I know people. Joe. I can look into the eyes of most of them and see just how their minds are workin'. And when I talked to Gabe tonight, I knew I was countin' on him to get himself killed. So maybe my life was on the line as well, Joe. Maybe if I'd got it wrong and he beat you – especially with that shitty shotgun trick which I never knew about – Gabe wouldn't have held back from blastin' me the way you did.'

He shook his head sharply again and was once more irritated with himself for drifting off the subject.

'Look, in a nutshell, I want you with me, Joe. And the hundred grand is just for starters. Name the figure you want me to pay you every month. Whatever kinda place you want to live in, I'll have it built. You can have the pick of the women in Elgin. Anything you've ever wanted anywhere, I'll have it shipped here for you –'

Edge had rolled a cigarette and now he lit it with a match struck on the butt of his holstered Colt as he stood up from the table. Put on his hat and buttoned his sheepskin coat. While the fat man watched him with a series of expressions that opened with surprise and ran through disappointment, despondency, anxiety, irritation and bitterness to the threshold of rage, which was about to be vented as the half breed said evenly:

'My soul is the same as my gun, feller. Not for sale. Either way.'

'Either way, Joe?' Gray's temper was off the boil, but reduced only to a simmer.

'To be used or put on ice.'

The fat man shook his head, so vigorously his flabby cheeks and many chins quivered. 'You don't understand, Joe. You won't be like Gabe Millard and the rest of the hired help. For you, it'll be like

76

you were Zach. Family – better than family. You won't be a hired hand, Joe. You and me'll be partners. What d'you say?'

'Want there to be just one thing between you and me, feller,' Edge said as he moved away from the table toward the arched doorway.

'Name it and you got it.'

'Distance.'

He opened the door and stepped out into the hallway that still smelled faintly of the smoke and steam and burnt oil of the doused fire in the sitting room. But also permeating the atmosphere were some pleasanter aromas – from the raven hair, beautiful face and slender body of Hedda Trask. Who had quite obviously been eavesdropping at the door and who now smiled her admiration for Edge around the finger she pressed to the centre of her half open lips.

'So beat it, you crazy bastard!' the fat man exploded. 'Get the hell outta my house, my town and my county. And stay a stinkin', penny-pinchin', ragged assed saddletramp for the rest of your shitty life, runt!'

The half breed closed the door quietly on the ranting man, whose voice could still be heard without the words sounding clearly enough to be understood.

The woman dropped her hand to her side and said softly against the distant ravings of Earl Gray: 'It's a real pleasure to meet a real man. Going to be worth suffering him in a temper after seeing somebody stand up to him. And I thought you were going to be like the rest of them.'

Edge took the cigarette from his lips, blew a stream of smoke toward the woman and growled:

'All it takes, lady, is to tell him no and walk away.'

He replaced the cigarette.

Hedda Trask's smile became hard and bitter and cynical as she rasped through her perfectly matched teeth: 'Anybody who ain't Zach Irish or you did that, mister, they'd be dead before they took two steps.'

Now every semblance of any kind of smile was gone from her face which suddenly was no longer beautiful as it showed a frown of evil cunning. 'And dead I don't wanna be. That has to be even worse than being poor. Rich is a whole lot better.'

Earl Gray had finished bellowing out his enraged tirade at the absent half breed and the woman with skin deep beauty lowered her voice in the utter silence that gripped the big, expensive, unhappy house.

'And I don't give a shit about what you think of me, mister. I got something he wants and as long as he keeps on paying high for it, I got no intention of turning my back on him.'

Edge made no reply and neither did he respond with a change in his impassive expression before he turned away from the woman and started along the hallway to the double doors, footfalls rapping on the polished flooring.

'Hedda!' Earl Gray roared.

Edge opened one of the front doors of the house and glanced back to see the woman grimace her revulsion and then wreath her face with a smile before she opened the door of the dining room. About to step out on to the terrace, the half breed paused: having glimpsed the start of a look of terror which again stripped Hedda Trask of beauty.

The crack of the gunshot was not loud. And the weapon was not powerful enough to explode the bullet out of her back after it had penetrated into her belly. And neither was the impact heavy enough to stagger her backwards across the hallway. So she merely stood in the open doorway for stretched seconds, staring into the room and then down at where blood was blossoming a stain on the front of her dark dress. Then brought her hands to the wound and took them away again – to peer incredulously at the stains upon them. Opened her mouth in a way that suggested she was going to utter beseeching words rather than to scream, before Earl Gray said in an ice cold tone:

'You maybe were tryin' to screw me blind, Hedda. But I ain't gone deaf.'

'No, Earl, please don't . . . ' she begged. And stepped backwards three paces while she stared wide eyed into the room. At the fat man who was close enough so that his ringed right hand fisted around the butt of a Remington over-and-under came into view beyond the door frame when he extended his arm to aim at her terror stricken face.

'Bitches are the same as dogs,' he cut in on her plea as she froze, perhaps three feet away from the twin muzzles of the .41 calibre handgun. 'When they're no longer loyal to their master, they have to be put down.'

She reached out with her bloodstained hands toward him, then knew she could expect no mercy from him and started to turn her head to direct a tacit plea at Edge. Whose ice blue eyes glinting through the screen of rising tobacco smoke offered her no hope. And an instant later, the second barrel of the small gun exploded a bullet. That went into the side of her head to drive through her brain – killed her on her feet and left a wound that was hidden by her hair as she sank to the floor and spasmed once before she became still.

The pudgy hand with its jewelled rings glittering in the overhead lights remained in view as its fist was unclenched so that the Remington could drop to the floor.

'Appreciate it if you'd close the door after you, Joe,' the fat man said dully as he slowly withdrew his hand from sight. 'Goin' to be cold in the house tonight.'

Edge shifted his gaze from the doorway of the dining room to the one beside the stairs at the rear of the hall, where the Chinese servants stood in a shocked and silent group: drawn there by the sound of gunfire.

'You're bound to feel the draught, feller,' he said evenly with the cigarette bobbing at the corner of his mouth. 'Without a woman to warm your bed and the place full of Chinks.'

Nine

PEARL Irish had taken the rockaway back to Elgin City after two of the Chinamen loaded the blanket wrapped corpse of Gabe Millard aboard it.

The country wagon with the canopy top was still parked at the foot of the steps from the terrace, but after giving it no more than a glance the half breed ignored the rig and started down the drive at an ambling walk, his booted feet crunching noisily on the gravel in the stillness of the night. Until the sound was masked by the louder ones of the wagon and horse moving from a standstill into a tight turn and then starting down the slope: the driver in no haste.

Edge took a few more paces and halted, having dropped the cigarette butt under his leading foot: then crushed out its fire as he turned to look back at the approaching rig: as seemingly indifferent to his surroundings as he had been since closing the door of the house. Seeing the driver as no more than a slightly built shadow against other shadows under the canopy.

'I don't mean you no harm, stranger,' Bob Lowell said nervously after he reined in the horse to stop the wagon alongside the silent half breed. 'Would've hid and took a shot at you if I did. Man like you that's faster than Gabe Millard was.'

'Long time since he was in Dodge, and he was out of practice, way the fat man told it,' Edge said.

'Like all of us. You wanna ride to town?'

'Walking's only good for bootmakers, feller,' Edge answered. 'Was hoping you were going to offer back there.'

He gestured with a thumb up the driveway as he climbed up into the rear seat of the wagon. Lowell caught his breath, then shrugged as he said in a melancholy tone:

'Yeah, Gabe had that way of tellin' when somebody was around even when there was no way of seein'.'

He clucked to the horse and remained silent while the hooves and wheel-rims crunched gravel. Then, when he had turned out of the Triple X entrance to head for town, asked:

'Am I right in thinkin' that was Mayor Gray's little pocket gun that was fired twice before you come out the house?'

'You're right.'

'Anybody hurt?'

'First he gut shot his woman. Then put one in her head. She hurt between times, I guess.'

'So you ain't gonna take Gabe's place?'

'It wasn't just from bad temper, kid. He heard her tell me she was using him.'

Lowell spat off the side of the wagon. And Edge had the impression that, just as the youngster sought to imitate the shrug of Millard, so he modelled the act of spitting on the way Chris Hite did it.

'Hot damn, he has to know all of us only take the shit he hands out on account of the high pay that comes with it. You made him killin' mad by not doin' what he wanted. If he wasn't that, he'd likely just have slapped her around some.'

'Kid?'

'Yeah?'

'You figure you can't beat me in a shoot out. So you plan to make me pine myself to death over some hard as nails ass peddler who knew the score when she laid it on the line for the fat man and –'

'Hot damn, stranger, I ain't blamin' you for nothin'!' Lowell cut in quickly and anxiously as he drove the rig by the town maker. 'Even if Gabe and me did warn you how the mayor would be if you turned him down, it was up to you what you done. Hell, no, I ain't sayin' it's your fault. Not none of it. I'm just speakin' aloud my thoughts, I guess. While I try to figure out what's best for me now that Gabe ain't around no more . . .

The remains of the gunfighter from Dodge City were still close by as the youngster who admired him so much spoke of him. For the freckle faced Sam Gower had not yet buried the corpse on an area of unfenced ground featured with several elongated humps out back of the undertaking parlour: the mortician still in process of digging another grave beside two only recently filled in – shovelling the displaced dirt to the sife of the deepening hole, across from where a plain pine coffin rested.

Gower's sweat sheened bald head reflected the moonlight as he laboured with the chore. And Bob Lowell uncovered his and broke off what he was saying until the country wagon rolled on to the western end of Elgin's main street and the blacksmith's forge blocked the view to the town's Potter's Field.

'Whether to stick around or to get out and give up

the whole idea of raisin' Herefords,' he went on. 'That's a breed of British cow me and Gabe was gonna run on some range he'd seen over in Minnesota Territory some place. After we'd made the money we needed from workin' for Mr Gray. Don't reckon I could cut it on my own. Probably be best to stick around. Watch my step and keep saltin' cash away until I can figure out somethin' else to do with my life.'

There was a gleam of light from a turned low lamp at the foot of the door to Sam Gower's premises. And some more showed at the windows of the Delaware Saloon and the office of the Elgin County Herald on opposite corners of the intersection. Every other building on both sides of the length of the town's main street was in total darkness. And there was just the thud of the shovel as it bit into the earth to compete with the clop, creak and rattle of the rig moving slowly over the hard packed surface.

'But it ain't gonna be easy for me, stranger,' Lowell went on, gazing directly ahead while Edge peered from side to side: surveying the many areas of moon shadow under sidewalk roofs and in alley mouths and scanning the uneven roof lines of the buildings. 'Not without Gabe around to keep tellin' me all the time how it's all gonna be worth it in the end. That it's not gonna matter, when we have the place over in Minnesota, that the mayor played with us like we was part of the biggest toy in the world – hot damn, what's that!'

Lowell reined the horse to a sudden halt and thrust forward his left arm, forefinger pointing. To single out from the night shrouded town a deeply shadowed strip of sidealk out front of the premises of a watch and clock repairer that was next to

Hedda's Hats: fifty feet in front and to the right of where he had stalled the rig.

Edge, having sensed the country wagon was under close scrutiny ever since it rolled in off the open trail, raked his gaze toward the area the young gunman indicated: having failed to see any sign of the secret watchers himself and thus certain he was not under imminent threat. But open to being proved wrong and clawing his right hand up from the seat to fist around the butt of the Frontier Colt.

Lowell was already rising from the driver's seat and powering off the wagon to the left by the time the half breed had focussed his slitted, glinting eyes on the dark façade of the store. And failed to see any shadow on shadow that rang a warning bell in his brain and caused him to draw the revolver and thumb back the hammer. But then, on the periphery of his vision as he made to shift his attention to the youngster scrambling off the rig, he saw the actual danger – as moonlight was reflected dully off something darkly metallic gripped in the right hand of Bob Lowell. The kid having brought in his pointing arm, curled the hand and drawn the Colt from his holster as he plunged to the side. Where he now hit the street, sure footed but the momentum twisting him from the waist so that he was unable for a stretched second to steady his aim as he thrust out the cocked gun at arms length.

'Gabe was – ' he started to scream shrilly.

'Hold it, kid!' a woman bellowed.

'Lowell, don't!'

'You crazy – '

'Don't be stu – '

Edge had planned his counter in the instant he saw the source of the danger. And readied his muscles to put it into effect in the next instant. This at the moment Lowell's feet made first contact with the street. And he was starting to power off the seat as the arm and hand and gun began to arc to draw a bead on him: the grief stricken screaming taunts of Lowell began and were almost immediately drowned by the cacophony of competing voices from the area of the intersection.

The burst of vocal sound took the younger man by surprise and momentarily distracted him. Which gave the half breed a sliver of time more to launch himself off the wagon – rising, turning and leaping in the same manner as Lowell. But in the opposite direction, and making no attempt to remain on his feet he hit the street.

Lowell wrenched his attention back to the rig, his round and button eyed face showing an expression fixed midway between the strange mixture of grief and triumph with which he had opened the move and one that was a mingling of fear and non-comprehension triggered by the sounds and sight further up the street.

He squeezed off a shot in a panicked reaction to the sudden tilt of the country wagon as the half breed shifted his weight. And the bullet cracked through the windowless body of the rig to thud into a sidewalk roof sign that advertised:

5c. PUBLIC BATH 5c.

Edge hit the street and pitched himself out full length alongside the wagon: on his side so that his right hip and shoulder took the jolting impact of the fall, while he held the Colt in a double handed grip – aimed under the vehicle between the leading and rear wheels. And triggered a shot that drilled a bullet into the crotch of the kid – just as the youngster was starting to drop to his haunches so that he could aim beneath the wagon.

The half breed's shot was one of a fusillade that crackled. To entirely drown out the groan of disappointment that Bob Lowell vented as he was bowled over backwards by the impact of the bullet: still gripping his Colt as he experienced the initial bolt of agony and clutched both hands to its source.

'You were good, kid,' Edge murmured as he thumbed back the hammer while Lowell went down on to his back: waiting for him to fold up into a seated posture so that he could blast a killing shot into a vital organ.

But then a single shot split the silence of the night in the area where the volley had been fired earlier. At the same moment as Lowell directed a shrill scream toward the moon. Which was the general direction in which the hail of bullets had been aimed, Edge saw, when he craned his neck to turn his head and peer along the street. To where a dozen men and the four daughters of Pearl Irish were grouped on the intersection, many with handguns and rifles still canted skywards through a slow drifting pall of acrid smoke. While, isolated at the front of the gathering, Elgin's woman sheriff had her revolver aimed from the hip, tilted slightly downward so that she continued to cover the divot her bullet had dug in the surface of the street. Just under the barrel of the half breed's gun. Which was an incredibly accurate shot over a distance of more than seventy feet.

'Anyone aims a gun at me now better kill me with it!' Edge shouted: able to keep the injured Lowell in blurred vision from the corner of his eye while he gazed at the group on the intersection.

'On your feet and on your way, Joe,' Pearl Irish

commanded harshly. 'And leave that creep for Elgin folks to deal with.'

She started along the street toward the halted rig between the public baths and a gunmaker's establishment with a man sprawled out to either side of it. And her daughters and the hard men trailed her, responding to her soft spoken command that they should holster their handguns and rest their rifles.

In the wake of his scream and the silence with which he had listened to the exchange between Edge and the woman sheriff, Bob Lowell began to moan. But in despair rather than pain. The half breed peered under the wagon at him and saw he had released his grip on the Colt as he struggled to sit up. And said, as he rose to his feet and slid his own gun into the holster:

'You really fooled me, feller. You should have taken up acting instead of gunslinging.'

'Not me, Mrs Irish!' the young man with the dark stained crotch rasped out through a throat dried by pain and terror. 'The stranger's the one you want! There was some more shootin' after you left and brought Gabe's body down to Sam Gower, ma'am! Two shots! Like maybe he blasted the mayor and the lady from the hat store, too. The stranger, he comes outta the house and says he'll kill me if I don't drive him down to town so he can get his horse and gear. Says I have to tell anybody that tries to stop him that the mayor give him the okay to leave and –'

Lowell screamed again – but in expectation of pain and subsequent evil rather than in response to it. The shrill sound started when Pearl Irish halted on a spot just inches from his head: and drew back a booted foot. And curtailed when her toe slammed into the side of his head, to plunge him into unconciousness.

The woman's entourage of daughters and gunmen had come to a halt in an uneven arc around the front of the horse in the traces – and either grinned or glowered silently at the injured and unconcious Lowell or the merely bruised and very much aware Edge.

Pearl Irish sighed softly and only now holstered her gun as she looked over the driver's seat of the country wagon and growled:

'Get while the gettin's good, Joe!'

'Hell, Mom, we didn't oughta let him just ride off until we're sure he didn't do Granddaddy no harm!'

'I ask for your advice, Anne Irish?' the oldest woman asked of the youngest, shortest and plumpest of her daughters.

'No, Mom, but I go along with – ' the prettiest girl started.

'Hush it up, Gloria,' the one Edge knew was named Laura said harshly – she had the kind of scowling face that suggested she might be incapable of speaking or acting in any other way. 'Let's get him strung up.'

'That's right,' the tall and almost skinny Joy agreed. 'Look, here comes Granddaddy now.'

Everyone peered along the street and out on to the moon whitened trail to where the unmistakable form of Earl Gray could be recognised on the seat of a buckboard being driven by one of his Oriental servants.

The pace was slow and there was no change in it when the approaching buckboard became, for a few moments, the centre of attention. Before, without any order being given, the group around the stalled country wagon suddenly broke up: the girl deputies and the hard men yelling raucously that the mayor was on his way into Elgin. Which brought a handful of men spilling out of the saloon and a larger crowd – men and women – from off the side street where they had apparently been drawn together by the gunfire of a few minutes ago. All of them to hurry to their respective business premises and light lamps.

Amid all this activity, just Edge, the town sheriff and the unconcious Bob Lowell remained unruffled beside the country wagon. While the buckboard rolled to the end of the street and was halted. And the fat man stayed seated aboard it as the Chinese climbed down, went to the rear, hefted something wrapped in a blanket over his shoulder and started in the direction of Elgin's Potter's Field.

'Who, Joe?' Pearl Irish asked dully.

'Hedda Trask. She said the wrong thing at the wrong time.'

'Shit! Dad really . . . Best you get movin', I think.'

He touched his hat and said: 'Obliged, ma'am. It's what I had in mind to do.'

'Damn you for bein' so much like my Zach!' she rasped, and viciously kicked Lowell's gun far out of the youngster's reach as he made the groaning sounds to announce that he was on his way back to conciousness.

This as Edge set off along the street busy with people hurrying to open and illuminate their places of business and a lesser number who were yelling at the rest to move faster. Every one of them taking a little time off from his or her pressing chore to direct a look of scowling resentment at the tall, lean, unresponsive half breed who ambled unswervingly down the centre of the street: apparently blaming him entirely for this new upheaval in the routine of this town.

'Don't make no odds to me, mister,' the short sighted and almost bald Devine murmured as he pushed open a door of his livery as Edge reached it. 'I live in a shack right out back of this place. But these surprise trips Mayor Gray makes to town at nights, they sure rile most folks hereabouts. Here's your mount, sir. Mrs Irish, she said you'd probably want him ready to leave. He's been fed, watered and curried so that'll be five dollars. There ain't no reduction for the animal bein' in a stall just part of a night.'

Edge listened patiently to the short, powerfully built, eye straining liveryman and when he was through opened a hand to show that he had the bill ready to pay for the stable service.

'Appreciate it, sir,' Devine said, his lens-magnified eyes and the set of his slack mouth expressing misery as he passed the reins of the ready-saddled bay gelding to Edge. 'Only wish I never had to charge so high.' He raised and lowered his broad shoulders as he stepped off the threshold to survey the street. 'But like I told you, Mr Gray takes a big part of – '

'That's right, feller, you did already tell me about your stable economy,' the half breed growled as he straightened from checking the tautness of the cinch. Then he swung up astride the saddle and directed his glinting, narrow eyed gaze along the street which just a few minutes earlier had been in near darkness: and was now bright with the glow of countless lamps.

'Wiley Reece that runs the wagon shop next door was only sayin' this mornin' how it's wrong we do all the heavy chores and the mayor just sits back and collects the lion's share of the reward. And that didn't oughta be, did it, mister?'

'It's because he knows a good ground rule, feller,' the half breed answered as he tugged gently on the reins to head the gelding eastward.

'Uh?' the liveryman grunted.

Edge jerked a thumb over his shoulder to indicate the brilliantly lit street stretched out behind him and explained: 'That many hands make light work.'

Ten

'EDGE, you sonofabitch!'

The slow riding half breed had not looked back as he took out the makings and rolled a cigarette: while the peace of Elgin City was disturbed only by the clop of the gelding's hooves and a distant murmuring of talk at the centre of town. Then the shrill, bitterly shouted words caused him to rein in the horse beside the marker just beyond the grade school that was on the north side of the eastern end of the main street – isolated by several vacant lots from its saddlery neighbour and the only building not illuminated. Where he struck a match on the stock of the Winchester jutting from the boot and lit the smoke before he turned in the saddle to show that he had heard Bob Lowell's commanding words.

And saw that the citizens of Elgin were being herded into an audience again and that once more the area where the two streets met was the stage for this new tableau of evil. The progress of which was temporarily halted by the shouting of the injured man and the tacit response of the mounted one at the end of the street.

Earl Gray was alone on the buckboard now, the wagon parked crosswise in front of the law office set back behind the gallows which were hidden to Edge's view by the bakery. Between the two horse team in the traces of the buckboard and the out of sight gallows stood the pretty Gloria Irish and her skinny sister, Joy. Each grasping a wrist of the hapless youngster who they had dragged, leaving a trail of blood, the seventy some feet from the point out front of the public baths where the half breed shot him down. Pearl Irish and her other two daughters were not to be seen. The section of the crowd gathered on the eastern side of the intersection had split to open up a gap through which Lowell, having forced his head up, and the turned in the saddle Edge, could see each other.

'They're gonna hang me, you cold as ice bastard!' the young gunman with the dark bruise on his temple shouted hoarsely. 'So I'm gonna be like Gabe! All our troubles'll be over with! But I hope you live to be a friggin' hundred and seventy, Edge! And I hope you never find what you're looking for and you go through friggin' livin' hell every –'

He was forced to end his tirade of sinister wishes for the half breed when, at a snarled command from Earl Gray, the two female deputy sheriffs stepped forward and into a turn. Triggering a fresh bolt of fiery agony from his gunshot crotch. And then, at the bidding of the grossly fat man, too, the audience which had split was abruptly melded into one again. And the sight of Bob Lowell being hauled toward the gallows where he was doomed to die was hidden from Edge. But the sound of the condemned man's suffering carried the length of the main street's eastern stretch and out on to the open trail where the half breed rode – calmly smoking a cigarette and expressing a total lack of feeling that was a true reflection of his thoughts.

Then either the pain became too much for Lowell's nervous system to continue to function and he was plunged into merciful unconciousness again, or the physical torture ceased and he was able to accept his fate stoically as he stood on the gallows. For the strident venting of his suffering was abruptly curtailed and for several seconds no sound in Elgin City was loud enough to reach out along the trail and compete with the even cadence of the gelding's easy moving hooves on the moonlit trail.

And the unshaven, travel stained man who rode easy in the saddle continued to be stone faced as his eyes raked back and forth along their glittering slits under the hooded lids – maintaining a cautious and yet effortless watch on the shadowed terrain he crossed.

A voice, too distant for words and therefore sense to be decoded from the mere sound of the man speaking, reached the half breed. But he could guess from the tone of exhortation discernible in the far off voice that a preacher was pleading Lowell's case to a higher authority than that of Earl Gray. But the fat man had total control over the immediate situation and his voice rang out clearly into the night as he bellowed across the prayer and ended it.

'Shit to all this spoutin' about souls, preacherman! I heard about souls already tonight and I don't wanna hear no more! Assholes is what they all are! Pull the lever, girl, and let's get it done with!'

There was a stretched second of utter silence in the chill Wyoming night. Then the steady clop of hooves sounded against a body of sound comprised of the gasps, sighs, subdued cries and small movements which were the responses of the watchers to the sight of Bob Lowell dropping through the suddenly opened trap and swinging at the end of the noosed rope.

Edge drew back his lips then, to display a cool smile of satisfaction that the man who had drawn twice against him and tried to kill him was now dead. But he did not gloat – even before the captive audience for the execution was ordered to disperse, the smile that never touched his eyes was gone and he was impassive again, calmly smoking and cautiosly watching the trail ahead and the country to each side of it. Occasionally and absently moving his left hand across his body to massage the aching areas at his right shoulder and hip which were bruised by his premeditated tumble from the country wagon. He did not look back.

The terrain to the east of Elgin City was more undulating than that which stretched westward toward the Sweetwater valley. Rockier and with more extensive stands of mixed timber. Maybe the soil was as rich, but the contours of the land made it more difficult to work and to keep tabs on livestock. And there was just an occasional isolated homestead within sight of the constantly turning, rising and falling trail: in darkness and with a cold chimney at this hour. The places lightly fenced to mark property lines rather than to keep animals out of the fields. The trail over which the rested horse was sometimes eager to move at a faster than walking pace was more heavily used than that which connected the Sweetwater River crossing with Elgin City.

And covered a broader area of land to the county line than did the western stretch. For the half breed had been two hours in the saddle – having ridden from the end of one day into the start of the next –

without seeing anything to suggest he was off the property of Earl Gray, when he heard a familiar sound from some way behind him: muted by intervening high ground. And angled the gelding to the right, down a slight, fifty feet wide incline and into the deep shadow of a wooded ravine mouth at the base of a twenty feet high, sheer faced bluff. There wheeled his mount into a half turn and stayed in the saddle, both hands holding the reins and draped over the horn as he waited and watched the point on the trail where the wagon hauled by two horses would first show.

It was another buckboard – this one not smelling of fresh creosote like that which had carried Chris Hite and Sam Tufts out to the Sweetwater crossing – but apparently employed for a similar purpose this side of town. For the rig, being driven at an unhurried pace, had two men in their mid-forties up on the sprung seat. One of them was tall and broad and the other, who drove, was tall and lean. Wrapped in thick coats against the chill bite of the night air and wearing low crowned, wide brimmed Stetsons. But riding toward the moon so that its light fell across their faces and Edge was able to recognise them – had seen both of them on the main street of Elgin City and between times engaged in a card game at the newspaper office on the mid-town intersection.

The both of them wore expressions of soured disillusionment, which hardened into scowls of fear backed aggression when the half breed heeled his horse forward and greeted:

'Morning.'

The thin man jerked the team to a halt and both of them snapped their heads around to stare at Edge. But were experienced enough at their trade to be aware that their holstered revolvers were inaccessible under the thick coats they wore. And so did not move their uncalloused hands. In the next moment recognised the moonlit man on the horse and expressed relief that he posed no threat of immediate harm before the former soured looks took command of their scrubbed and shaved features again.

While, during this same period, Edge verified his intial estimation about the men's purpose and decided it was no part of their early hours mission to cause him trouble.

The broadly built man growled: 'Go to hell, mister!' Shifted his gaze to the trail ahead and ordered: 'Move it out, Jesse.'

'Yeah, Edge or Hedges or whatever your name is,' the driver added in a complaining tone as he flicked the reins over the backs of the two chestnut geldings, 'you stirred up enough shit in town. Least you can do is keep clear of me and Cleve out here.'

Edge gave a slight nod of acknowledgement as the buckboard rolled away from him and he moved on to the trail behind it – the driver and passenger facing front again. The team and the saddle horse making the same easy pace as before the meeting.

'One thing.'

'Yeah?' the powerfully built Cleve asked without turning around.

'Far to the county line?'

'No more than fifteen minutes at this speed, mister. You could make it a whole lot faster ridin' a horse.'

'Obliged.'

He did not swing to the side and demand a faster pace from the gelding. And after he had been trailing the buckboard for another hundred yards or so,

Jesse found the vocal silence disconcerting. Allowed:

'Reckon you can't help what happened, mister.'

He drew no response as Edge took out the makings to roll a cigarette and Cleve continued to scowl sourly between the gently nodding heads of the team horses.

Jesse went on: 'Killin' the guy that knifed Zach Irish and bein' like Zach is just somethin' that happened –'

'He don't look like the picture Pearl Irish has got of the guy she was married to,' Cleve said, and glanced over his shoulder as Edge heeled his mount closer to the buckboard, angled to the side of it and extended a hand toward the offside rear wheel. So that the match he held was ignited by the slow turning rim and he was able to light the cigarette.

'Guess Irish didn't lick the fat man's ass,' the half breed said evenly on a trickle of smoke.

'Jesus, I bet you didn't call Mr Gray that to his face when –'

'What the frig does it matter, Jesse?' the forward facing bigger man cut in dully on the driver who had wrenched around on the seat to hurl the challenge at Edge. 'And we'll have the last laugh on this guy, anyway. When we've all made our piles and are sittin' pretty some place. And he's still saddletrampin' around worried about where his next bite to eat is comin' from.'

In its own, less direct way, this was also a verbal gauntlet thrown down for the half breed to pick up. Edge gave no indication that he had heard what was said and after several seconds of vain waiting, the man went on:

'Sure Jesse Antrim here, and me and the rest of

the boys on his payroll, let Earl Gray treat us like we're no better'n them Chinese he's got workin' for him down at the house. But pride slides down easy when the money's so friggin' good, mister. And when everyone's treated the same. Say what you like about Earl Gray, he don't play no favourites. Hands out the high price shit to everybody the same. So everybody knows where he stands.'

'It's how he falls where the surprises come,' Edge said now. 'Down dead.'

Cleve shook his head without turning around as he corrected: 'No, mister. There's rules about that in Elgin County. Strangers that get outta line have to go up against Earl Gray the way you saw it happen with them two cowpunchers that didn't buy a pass and bad mouthed two of the Irish girls. Local folks are usually strung up the way that crazy kid was tonight.'

'Crazy is right,' Antrim put in balefully. 'If Bob Lowell had bushwhacked you out in the country and told his tale, he could've got away with it, Cleve. I figure. But he had to try for that grandstand play.' He looked over his shoulder at Edge. 'Prove to everybody he was good enough to take over the top spot from his dead buddy, Gabe Millard. The kid told Mr Gray that when Mr Gray said that if he didn't get the truth, he was gonna pour salt on the wound where you shot his balls to bits, mister.

'Course, even if the kid had pulled it off, he wouldn't have been paid so much as his buddy was,' Antrim went on after a sniff and he concentrated on the trail ahead again. 'Gabe Millard got top money for not wearin' his gun except when Mr Gray told him. On account of Mr Gray likes to be the fastest around.'

There was another pause in the talk with which all three men seemed comfortable. Until Cleve revealed that something had been irking him, when he said malevolently:

'It's the business people in town and the home-steaders and hands on the Triple X range that suck up to him, mister! To stay in business or keep their jobs. Cleve Sterlin' ain't never licked no man's ass. Sells his gun to the highest bidder, that's all. Because that's the quickest way he knows to get a stake to take care of him in his old age. And in this business, a man gets old quicker than in any of the others.'

'And I figured you were in the newspaper business,' Edge said as he ceased his broad, wide ranging survey of the landscape to either side of the trail and peered directly ahead. Beyond the few yards in front of the team horses where Jesse Antrim was morosely gazing. And while Cleve Sterling delved a hand into a deep pocket of his coat to bring out a bottle – which he uncapped and raised to his lips, tilting back his head to drink.

'The mayor had a shoot out with the guy that wrote the County Herald and the guy that ran the press, mister,' Sterling answered as he paused in sucking from the bottle and did not recap it. 'Crazy sonofabitch of a newspaperman tried to stir up folks against us. So him and the guy that printed the garbage got blasted into the cemetery. And me and Jesse and most of the boys started to bunk in the newspaper buildin'. Whole lot cheaper than the hotel. For nothin', you see.'

The bigger built man on the buckboard had held his liquor well until he took the long swig from the bottle. Now with fresh whiskey hitting and mixing with old, he began to slur his words and to sway from side to side and back to front. He raised the bottle again but this time tilted it instead of his head – to sip rather than gulp the liquor.

Edge remained aware of what was taking place close by while he continued to rivet a large part of his attention on a shack at the side of the trail that had been perhaps a half mile away when he first saw it. The frame building, that was about the same size as the one on the bank of the river at the western extent of Elgin County, sited on the south side of the trail across from an extensive stand of cottonwoods. A five strand barbed wire fence strung on six feet high poles spaced thirty feet apart stretched south from the far rear corner of the shack.

The building, the trees and the ugly fencing that marked the Elgin County line in the east were at the narrow end of what had started out as a broad valley with gently sloping, lushly green sides patterned with many stream beds that were mostly dry at this late fall time of year. Then, as the flanking slopes steepened to narrow the valley, so the bottom land between became more rugged and the vegetation more sparse. And in many places, the slopes had been scoured by rain and melt water and eroded by wind down to bare rock.

Beyond the county line at the mouth of the valley was a high plain that looked as barren and desolate as an arid south western territories desert in the cold, blue light of the early hours moon.

'You didn't oughta drink so much, Cleve,' Antrim warned, almost diffidently.

'I gotta have somethin' to get the taste outta my mouth, buddy,' the bigger man excused between sips. I should've got the top spot. Not that creep Hite!' He made sure he had emptied his mouth of whiskey before he worked some saliva up from his throat: and spat as forcefully as Hite usually did. 'With that kinda money I could've looked forward to hookin' them big fish outta the Gulf off my own boat before this friggin' year was through!'

The shack showed no light at either a window or the crack at the foot of the door. No smoke curled from its chimney on the far side. And no sound emerged from inside as the gap was narrowed between the newcomers and the building. Which was apparently normal for it did not arouse any apprehension in Cleve Sterling or Jesse Antrim. But one of them was in a state of liquor sodden depression while his partner appeared to be solely concerned with talking him out of it.

Edge sensed a threat and became increasingly more certain that something was wrong with each yard he closed in on the darkened and silent shack. But from the moment he first tensed to respond to whatever danger proved to lurk in the area of the eastern entrance to Elgin County, the only cover close at hand had been the insubstantial buckboard. Then the shack itself on one side of the trail and the expanse of cottonwoods on the other got invitingly closer by the moment.

'Cleve wants to be a boat fisherman outta Texas and I wanna buy me a –'

The door in the trail facing front of the shack swung open on creaking hinges as the driver of the buckboard prepared to haul on the reins and halt the rig and his passenger tilted both head and bottle to suck the last of the whiskey down his throat. And Edge shifted his feet, took a tighter grip on the reins and tensed his muscles to the limit as he made ready to demand a half turn and gallop into the trees.

'Hey, you guys!' Antrim greeted the unseen occupants of the shack after he broke off from the earlier topic. 'Have we got some hot news to tell you! Get the lamp lit and the stove fire started! Tell you all about it while we're eatin' supper . . . Aw, Jesus!'

'Christ, Jesse!' Sterling groaned.

The driver had stopped the buckboard and finished winding the reins around the brake lever, and his passenger had lowered the drained empty bottle into his lap before they spoke the blasphemies. Their gasping shock triggered by what was hanging on the inside of the shack's door – not seen until it had swung all the way open to fold against the front wall of the building. Into a position where the moonlight shone on two corpses. Which hung upside down and side by side on hooks designed to be draped with hats and coats. But tonight they were draped with the ropes which bound the ankles of the men. Who were obviously dead, because of the bloodied holes in their shirt fronts and the glazed stares in their eyes.

For perhaps one complete second there was total silence: as if the heartbeat of the entire world had suddenly stopped. Then a barrage of gunfire exploded out of the cottonwoods. To spray a hail of bullets at the buckboard from the muzzles of at least a dozen repeating weapons. The lead ripping into and out of the flesh of the bulky Cleve Sterling and the lean Jesse Antrim. Catching the men as they started to rise in a desperate and doomed attempt to escape. Flinging them back down on to and across the seat, huddled together. Both killed by the first volley, but the ambushers in the timber not satisfied by the stark act of a double killing: needing to pour more bullets into the unfeeling flesh or their victims, until their guns rattled empty or they were drained of the emotional stimulus that powered their vengeful hatred. And so the shooting came to a faltering end – the crackle of the reports, the stabs of the muzzle flashes and the acrid intensity of the black powder smoke lessening by degrees. Until a final shot sounded in isolation, to point a streak of flame at the huddled bodies into which the bullet drove: and to add for a moment a stronger pungency to the drifting, dispersing smoke.

After which, in the seemingly unnatural peace and quiet of the mouth of the valley, the team horses ceased to struggle in the traces of the buckboard with the brake on and Edge remained in his frozen attitude astride the gelding. His right hand fisted around the Winchester half drawn from the boot and the no longer smoking cigarette angled from a corner of his mouth – in all other respects still tensely poised to lunge his mount toward the shadowed timber in which so many gunmen were hidden. While his ice cold gaze shifted back from the trees to peer at the dark entrance to the shack beyond the fully open door with the men hanging upside down on it.

Where a man appeared, a tuneless whistle trickling through his pursed lips as he stepped across the threshold into the moonlight: a Winchester rifle in a one handed grip aimed from his hip in the general direction of the half breed. His left hand was down at his side, holding something that was in the shadow of his tall and broadly built body.

'The boys and me don't mean any harm to anyone who don't mean us harm, mister. Have to figure that if you don't let go of the rifle and get down off the horse that you've got evil intent toward us. In which case, you'll make five.'

He started the tuneless whistling again as he moved the rifle to use it as a pointer – to indicate the dead men on the door and aboard the wagon. Then angled it up at the mounted half breed again. While this mime with its almost musical accompaniment was taking place, the men in the timber thumbed back hammers and worked the actions of their revolvers and rifles: or cursed the emptiness of their guns and hurried to reload them.

Edge waited until the metallic sounds were ended and there was just the whistling of the man out front of the shack to disturb the silence. Then he unclenched his right hand to allow the rifle to slide fully back into the boot. While he drew his booted foot from the right stirrup and said:

'Have this thing about guns that are – '

'Aimed at you,' the man who had been whistling put in. 'You're well known for killin' men who do it twice after you've warned them the once. You wanna get off the horse or you wanna be dead?'

The half breed swung easily out of the saddle, tracked by the Winchester of the man who had tired of his whistling. While other sounds came from the timber – of booted feet disturbing the rotted leaves of many falls and sometimes snapping a dried, long dead twig.

'Match,' Edge announced flatly as a line of men materialised on the trail from the inky black backdrop of shadow beneath the cottonwoods and he brought up his right hand toward the lapels of his coat. Delved through and into a pocket of his shirt to bring out a match.

'German sausage,' the man at the doorway of the shack countered. And brought up his left hand to his face. Bit off a mouthful of meat.

Edge struck the match on the rear wheelrim of the buckboard and touched the flame to the half smoked cigarette. His eyes in their slits glittered coldly in the flaring light as he surveyed the line of thirteen men who covered him with revolvers held out at arm's length and rifles levelled from the shoulder. Then blew out a stream of tobacco smoke through clenched teeth bared in a mirthless grin and rasped:

'Yeah, feller. Looks like the wurst is yet to come.'

Eleven

THE man who liked to whistle but could not carry a tune was named Irwin Kansler, and like twelve of the thirteen men who emerged from the stand of timber, he was a farmer who once worked a homestead in Elgin County. The odd man out was Prentice Gilmore who owned the feed and seed store in town.

Gilmore was the oldest of the bunch at something over sixty. And wore glasses with lenses not near as thick as those needed by the Elgin City liveryman. But a weakening of his eyes appeared to be the only debilitating process of advanced years that affected him. For he was as powerfully built and looked as capable of taking care of himself in a tough situation as the others, who ranged in age from the mid-thirties to early fifties and were of mixed statures, not one of them suggestive of weakness.

Kansler was about fifty: a thick bodied, short necked, neatly black bearded man who was the undisputed leader of the group. He it was who named himself and Gilmore after he instructed the older man to take the Frontier Colt from the half breed's holster. Next named each of the other men – all attired in warm coats and hats with earflaps – as Edge unfastened his coat buttons and allowed the scowling Gilmore to take the revolver. They all scowled, too, although some nodded at the prisoner as the introduction was made. Their guns never wavered from the aim until after the sallow skinned Gilmore backed away from Edge with the confiscated Colt in his pocket.

Then, as the rest of the men made preparations to finish what had been so lethally started, Kansler gestured for Edge to step to the side of the trail and ambled over to join him. The still cocked Winchester held in a negligent attitude down at his side as he chewed with relish on the sausage and explained with his mouth full that one of the men was a storekeeper while the others were homesteaders.

'Prentice is the only feller still has actual connections with the place now,' the calmly speaking, totally unruffled man who was a head shorter than Edge went on as he leaned against a corner of the shack. 'Me and the rest of the boys, we been gone from Elgin County for five, six, seven years. Dependin' on how long each of us put up with havin' the fat man bleed us white.'

He finished the last of the sausage, licked his lips and asked: 'Don't guess no one around town told you about the boys and me?'

The bodies of Sterling and Antrim had been hauled off the buckboard and into the shack. They left a trail of blood from the multiple wounds. Gilmore was one of the three men who used handfuls of decomposing leaves from among the trees to clean the blood off the seat of the wagon.

'Guess they all had more important things on their minds, feller,' Edge answered as he watched his horse being hitched to the tailgate of the buckboard and heard another mount being brought from deep in the stand of cottonwoods.

Kansler grinned as he produced an already filled pipe from a pocket of his coat and leaned his rifle against the front wall of the shack as he lit the aromatic tobacco in the bowl.

'Always was the idea since we first started to plan this, Edge. You like Edge better than Hedges or what?'

The half breed still had the razor in the sheath at the nape of his neck. And the Winchester propped against .the wall on the other side of where Irwin Kansler stood was temptingly accessible. But the odds were too loaded against him and, he felt certain, these men were fanatical in their aims – would not hesitate to sacrifice the life of one of their own kind if it were necessary. So not even Kansler would serve as a hostage and thus the half breed had to submit to remaining one – for now.

'Josiah C. Hedges doesn't exist any more, feller,' he answered. And harboured a brief memory of five days he had spent on the shore of Mirror Lake in the north of Montana. Working the claim of a dead man with just the dead man's dog for company. A period of peace and contentment before violence shattered what was close to being an idyll and set him riding trails that brought him to Elgin County. A time during which Josiah C. Hedges was almost reborn, as he had been when the man called Edge met and married Beth many trouble filled years before.

'Okay, so Edge,' Irwin Kansler agreed readily as the half breed dropped the long butt of the cigarette and stepped on it – like it had suddenly started to taste bad. 'Me and the boys are gonna get back what us and our families was forced to give up when Earl Gray got land hungry. And I guess you don't need no tellin' that you're gonna lend a hand. Or the borrowed time you been livin' on for so long is gonna get called in.'

'Set to leave, Irwin!' one of the younger men, named Gerry Saxon, announced as he hauled himself up on to the buckboard seat and unfurled the reins from around the brake lever. His moves adroit despite the fact that all the fingers and part of the thumb on his left hand had been sheered off in a long ago accident.

'You ride up alongside Gerry,' Kansler instructed, gesturing with the stem of his pipe as he retrieved the Winchester and used its barrel to swing the shack door with its appendant corpses closed. Explained for anybody who cared to listen as he went to where Gilmore was holding his horse: 'Wouldn't want to scare any passin' through folks who came by. Fat chance.'

He was the last of the bunch to mount up, as Edge climbed aboard the wagon and lowered himself on to the seat beside the sullen faced driver whose horse was also hitched on behind the rig.

'Okay, Irwin?' Saxon asked while the buckboard remained at a halt, facing east toward the group of grim faced mounted men who were all headed west.

'Somethin' you should keep in mind, Edge,' Kansler said in the same slow and evenly pitched voice as always. 'You're an extra we never counted on havin'. So if you try anythin' tricky, it won't make much of a differnce to anybody that you'll be a dead duck. Except to you, of course.'

He showed a brief, sardonic smile but everyone else continued to express varying degrees of bitterness as the stem of the pipe was rotated in the air and Saxon set the buckboard moving, steering the team into a tight turn. To lead the way back along the trail toward Elgin City. All the riders save one staying in a loose knit bunch behind the rig. Kansler spurred his mount forward to ride alongside the buckboard, level with Edge. Who, together with the morose and taciturn driver, gazed fixedly ahead.

'It's my opinion that Gray's insane now,' the man astride the horse said through his teeth clenched to the pipe. 'He wasn't when he first came to this part of the country. Was a rich man and a good neighbour. Helped a lot of folk in troubled times. But wanted too much in return. Not money. Never charged no more than the goin' rate in interest for loans. Wanted what he called respectfulness. And what we simple folks reckon to be bowin' and scrapin'. You know what I mean, Edge?'

'If I don't, I also don't give much of a damn, feller.'

'You don't have to take that from him, Irwin!' Saxon snarled.

'Why don't I, Gerry?'

'Why? Because we got the upper hand here and he didn't oughta treat us like we're so much friggin' dirt, is why!'

'To Edge that's what we are,' Kansler answered evenly after taking the pipe from his mouth. 'If I ever do anythin' that earns me a higher opinion in his eyes, fine. But even then I won't lose no sleep if he don't kiss my ass.'

Saxon considered he had been quietly bawled out and he sank into a deeper ill humour when he faced front again. This as Kansler knocked burnt ash from the bowl and put the pipe back in his pocket before he took up his story again.

'Gray settin' up his ranchin' business outside of

Elgin did a lot for the town in the early days and anyone that denies it is a liar. It was him paid for the buildin' of the new church and the meetin' hall. The baths and the schoolhouse, he had built from nothin'. And it was a pretty damn good town to live in. Or for us that lived outside of it to come visit for business, pleasure, churchgoin' or whatever. And lotsa folks from way outside the county used to visit, too. On the Western Stage Line stages that used to run from Casper to Fort Bridger and Ogden. Good for business and good for folks in general to see other folks.'

He broke off to spread a pensive expression over his bearded face and to give a rueful shake of his head. 'I'll tell you, Edge, back then we was all of us eager for you to come ridin' into Elgin just to make Gray happy. Why, any one of us who had to take a trip would always make a point of lookin' at strangers to see if they matched up to the likeness Earl Gray showed all of us.

'But then it all turned sour. Wasn't no sudden, overnight change. Happened gradual, like. And I can see the man's point of view. A little. Nobody wanted his help anymore. All the loans were paid back and the folks that wanted more than they had didn't want to get it on credit. Wanted to work for it and earn it. And Earl Gray was just a bloated rich man who lived in the mansion on the hill. Without any power over anyone except his chink flunkies and the punchers that ran his herds on the Triple X spread. And that didn't set well with him. Bein' the kind of man he is.'

The buckboard with the two saddle horses hitched to the rear and its escort of riders was rolling through the broad section of valley now, over even ground between gentle slopes of lush pastureland. The stink of black powder smoke, freshly spilled blood and hours old death was not present in the clear, cold early morning air that was totally still upon this moonlit landscape. Elgin City was more than an hour and thirty minutes away at this unhurried pace and Irwin Kansler was in no rush to get his tale told. During this pause seemed to be taking the time to relish the pastoral scents and scenes: and to be listening with pleasure to the creak of wagon timbers, the rumble of the turning wheels and the clatter of many hoofbeats on the hard packed surface of the trail.

'First he got feisty with everyone over the least little thing. Then he started to stay at his house for days at a time. Then he took off on the Casper bound stage and was gone a month. When he came back, had title to every square inch of Elgin County that wasn't already settled. Includin' even this trail that we're ridin' over now. It was right about then he started to go off his rocker, seems to me. Power mad, like. Can you understand how the men that run the Territory can let one man get so friggin' much for himself?'

'There's a word for it, feller,' Edge said.

'There is?'

'Money.'

'Didn't come back with just a box of land titles, stranger,' Saxon put in, proving he had not been entirely wrapped up with introspective thoughts while he peered intently ahead. 'Had four mean lookin' and mean actin' hard men along with him.'

He spat forcefully off the side of the buckboard.

'Started to get back whatever it cost him,' Kansler said in a slightly miffed tone, like he was irritated the younger man had tried to take over his role as

114

the teller of the tale. 'To charge strangers a toll to use the trail.'

'But you didn't have to pay no toll?' Saxon growled. 'Seein' how that barrel of lard figures the sun shines outta your ass?'

'No help, feller. Yesterday I had to buy a ticket to ride across Elgin County. Was planning on it being just the one way.'

Kansler had started his tuneless whistling again, the set of his eyes revealing his impatience with Saxon. When the half breed was through with answering the younger man's point, he grimaced and rasped:

'It don't much matter what you think about what me and the boys are doin' tonight, Edge. But I don't hold nothin' against you on account of what I've heard about you and what Earl Gray's opinion of you is.' Abruptly he hardened his tone and snapped his head around to peer at the moon shadowed, heavily bristled profile of the half breed. Snarled: 'Don't hand me that one way crap, mister! Prentice told us about the hundred grand Gray deposited in your name at the town bank! And that'd be just the start for the man that killed the one stuck a knife in Zach Irish! Whatever you was doin' out at the county line tonight with Sterlin' and Antrim, it sure as hell wasn't ridin' out on a hundred grand down payment on –'

His voice was getting louder and its tone shriller. But he abruptly realised he was losing control of himself, ended what he was saying and licked his lips, blinked several times and glanced furtively about – like he was ashamed of the outburst and anxious that only the two men closest to him had heard it. More importantly, did not want anyone to realise that the strident diatribe was a symptom of fear: a humiliating dread of what was to come that he was only able to suppress with talk. Needing to concentrate his entire attention on a quiet discourse that allowed for no unasked for interruptions.

'Seems that Zach Irish and me had one thing in common that causes the fat man to figure I'm exactly like he was, feller. Zach's widow, too, come to think of it. He was a man without a price, same as me.'

Irwin Kansler had calmed himself, content that nobody had seen through the façade of the angry outburst to the shameful sense of foreboding beneath. For the men he led merely nodded their agreement with his estimation of Edge's motives. While the half breed remained impassive during the pause. And was just as emotionless as he spoke the rebuttal, in a way that provoked the bearded homesteader again but on this occasion with justification, he felt.

'You ain't alone in that!' he rasped and made the effort to force down the lid on his urge to rage. Started to talk in the slow and even tone that was natural to him. 'I already told you Elgin folks called a halt to the easy life Gray was givin' them at the beginnin'. Which is what led to the trouble.

'Pretty soon, the word was spread about the money it cost to cross Elgin County and folks stopped visitin'. Which wasn't good for business in town. And next Gray's hard men started to charge for us homesteaders to use the trail to reach town. And townspeople to use it for leavin'.'

'Had more men – ' Gerry Sutton started to say, but was driven to finish in mid-sentence by the glowering look Kansler directed at him.

'Had more men to turn the screws by then, Edge,'

the bearded rider of the horse beside the buckboard said as the trail crested a rise and the first of the isolated homesteads on the undulating terrain to the east of Elgin City could be seen – the darkened house with the cold chimney a mile or so to the right.

'That was Clay and Cathy Averill's place,' Kansler said. And then hurried on, as if afraid he might become maudlin. 'Had more men he paid big money to so he could work them like marionettes. And made his daughter woman sheriff and her four bitches of daughters the deputies.' He waved a negligent hand gesture to the left. 'House of the people work them fields is in the trees at the top of the hill. Was Charlie and Lil Bonham's place.'

Both Averill and Bonham were in the grim faced bunch riding in the wake of the slow rolling buckboard. A group of men who, like Irwin Kansler and Gerry Saxon, were noticeably infected by a rancorous wistfulness for times past as they entered once familiar territory.

Their bearded leader shook his head vigorously, as if it required such a physical action to rid himself of futile nostalgia and growled: 'Upshot was, us and a lot more folks cleared out. Fed up with havin' to pay up, or gettin' beat up or locked up in the gaolhouse Gray had specially built for Pearl Irish and them bitch daugthers of hers.

'Ain't none of us proud of pullin' out that way. But fact is, we done it. Because we couldn't afford to live in the kinda place Gray was runnin'.' And we didn't have the will to try to change it. Not when Gray had all the right bits of paper that said he was entitled to do what he was. And hired hands like them back there to stomp on anyone that even looked like complainin'.'

He jerked a thumb over his shoulder to indicate the far distant shack at the county line in which the corpses of four of Earl Gray's men were stored.

'But we got the will now, Irwin,' Saxon said with a note of excitement. And he gestured with his mutilated hand toward a homestead left of the trail. 'That was Susan's and mine in the old days, stranger. Will be again after tonight.'

On this occasion, Kansler made allowances for the intrusion. Said without a hint of irritation: 'Some of us had the idea for this way back, Edge. When we used the money Gray paid us for our places to start over again up there south of Casper. But there was just Gerry and me and Seth Corey and Roy Washington then. Not enough of us and we were too busy gettin' our new start.

'But gradually more and more folks took the money Gray offered them and left the county. Townspeople and homesteaders alike. And they all came through Casper on the way out. Some to stay and some to head for parts more distant from Elgin County. Which was gettin' worse and worse by the day by all accounts. With shootin's and lynchin's and Gray actin' like God Himself.'

'Satan more like, Irwin.'

'Yeah, Gerry. Anyway, the more we heard, the more we started to think how lucky we was to get out when we did. Until we thought around in a full circle and realised how friggin' gutless we been. On account of we was in this piece of country first and was doin' real fine without Gray. And we'd let the bastard squeeze us off of good land and on to places that didn't produce nearly half as well. So he could rent out our places to folks that knew the score and was ready to play it his way.

'And that's the long and the short of it, Edge. Prentice Gilmore, he's been keepin' us up to date with how things are when he visits in Casper to buy stock of feed and seed for his store. And he reckons the time is right to make our move – now that Elgin folks that have been here since before Gray came and them that have come in to take our place are near the end of their tethers. Be ready and willin' to turn on the hard men and the women with badges. And Gray. If we start things rollin'.'

'And we done that, Irwin,' Saxon said in a tone of hushed excitement now, as the town came into view in the far distance. And he was afraid a raised voice would carry through the silence of this early morning hour to reach the shadows upon shadows that was all Elgin City appeared to be from this range. 'Put four of his hired guns out of the way already. Just leaves a dozen more and two of them'll be out at the Sweetwater crossin'. Couple more line ridin' up in the north and down south, maybe. And the Irish crowd and the fat slob himself, of course.'

The man's mouth formed into the line of a grin of exhilaration as he spoke. And then, as he finished, an involuntary laugh of high glee burst from between his exposed clenched teeth.

'And with Edge's life to bargain with, I figure we're home and dry. Way Gray was always runnin' off at the mouth about him like he was a long lost son.'

The half breed had inched close to the brink of an abyss of blind anger while he sat the gelding during the explosion of gunfire that riddle two men with bullets. But that brand of rage held on the shortest of reins had been directed inward: as he realised he had made a mistake by which he deserved to die. When

119

he concentrated his entire attention on the shack where he sensed there was danger and, further, allowed himself to be fooled by the distraction of the creaking open door. Totally ignoring the timber as a place of possibly greater danger while he considered it only as a refuge.

For a long time, while preparations were made to leave the scene of the violence and then during the return trip, Edge was concerned almost exclusively with calming his nerves which had been set to jangling by the error he made. So that he had only half-heartedly considered making a try for Irwin Kansler's rifle back at the shack. And had listened with scant attention to the man who sought to justify himself and the evil he had perpetrated and intended to commit by cataloguing the evil deeds of his enemy.

Perhaps, after a protracted period of self-analysis, the half breed might have been able to fabricate an excuse for himself and next assuaged his damaged self-assurance with a vow he would never be so careless again. But Gerry Saxon's blandly spoken assessment of how he rated simply as a helpless hostage served to jerk Edge from his near fugue state.

He revealed no clue to his change of attitude, though — he gave no sign that a different brand of rage was reaching the ice cold point of explosion deep inside him. Not directed inward. And the movement of his right hand from out of his pocket to his face, there to scratch with all the fingernails at the bristles on his cheek, appeared as nothing more than the action of a man with a not very irritating itch.

The eastern fringe of the totally darkened Elgin City was still in the region of two miles away across the moonlit landscape. And daybreak was a lot further to the east than this. As Irwin Kansler peered for stretched seconds toward the town, then turned in the saddle to use as much time surveying the distant horizon at the rear – like he was making a fine estimation of a critical time factor.

'I ain't so sure, Gerry,' the bearded man muttered doubtfully, 'Maybe it wasn't such a great idea after all.'

'What d'you mean, Irwin?'

'That maybe he told the truth, Gerry. Maybe he was ridin' away from the offer Gray made him. Which won't be settin' right with the fat sonofabitch. And so he won't give a damn about us havin' Edge as a hostage.'

'So what's the difference, Irwin?' Saxon countered quickly, his excitement still high. 'We didn't know he was gonna show up in Elgin when we planned this for tonight. And even when Prentice came out and told us he was comin' to town, it didn't alter not a thing. He was just one more hard man we had to take care of. It was only when you saw him ridin' out with Sterlin' and Antrim you switched the plan. So we can dump him right here and go ahead like we was goin' to at first, seems to me.'

Edge shifted his right hand from his cheek to his neck. And altered its movement from a scratching to a massaging action – like he was rubbing at aching muscles.

'We still got the time, Irwin,' Saxon went on eagerly. 'Still far enough outside of town. Ain't nobody heard us comin'.'

The half breed's long, brown skinned fingers moved slowly back and forth against his skin under the ends of his hair at the back as he said in a weary tone that seemed to hold in a yawn: 'I hope he don't

121

mean by dump what he could mean by it, feller?'

'Well, you gotta see it from our viewpoint, Edge. Tales that been comin' to Elgin about you for so long, you ain't the kinda guy to let somethin' like this pass by without doin'–'

'Dump as in what folks do with garbage. The stuff that gets to stink when it's kept around too long. And the only thing to do with it is get rid of it –'

The half breed tried to the limit of his capability to control his rage: to confine it to an ice cold ball – much like fear – at the pit of his stomach. But he failed, dismally.

And thereby survived.

Gerry Saxon was smirking to express the kind of triumph that only a man who knows he has beaten much greater odds can experience. Relishing every word he spat out, the sound of each one heightening his enjoyment of a situation in which it was impossible for him to conceive defeat.

Edge saw the look on the man's face for just a moment from the left corner of his slitted left eye. Then raked his eyes along their sockets to glimpse the apologetic look on the face of the bearded man riding the horse.

Gaped his wide, thin lipped mouth open to its widest extent. Which Saxon thought was the prelude to a cry of despair and caused him to curtail his taunts. But instead, what was vented from deep within the half breed was a roar like that of some gigantic wild animal that has found voice after a lifetime of anguished muteness. Which triggered panic in the minds of the horses and deeply shocked the men. Including Edge himself. But neither the traumatic experience of discovering he was capable of such an act, nor the abrupt lunge into a bolt by the two horses drawing the buckboard hampered him in bringing the straight razor out of the neck pouch. And arcing it, tightly clenched in his right fist, across the front of his body and toward Gerry Saxon.

Whose smirk of triumph was in process of altering to a mask of terror as he heard the animalistic bellow and saw the sudden move. Gaped his own mouth wide and abandoned the reins of the bolting team in a desperate attempt to bring up his hands and defend himself against his assailant. And quite possibly died without being aware that Edge was attacking him with more than just a fist. For the honed point of the razor penetrated his left eyelid, the eye itself and the tissue behind it to find the brain and kill the man all in just part of a second that allowed no time for even subconscious thought.

The buckboard was already picking up sudden speed as Edge jerked the length of the blade out of the head of the dead man: powered by the two terrified horses in the traces and unhindered by the pair of equally frightened animals hitched on at the rear. The momentum forced the limp form of Saxon back against the back of the seat. Then he was knocked sideways by Edge as the half breed grabbed for and held on to the reins just as they were about to slide off the knees of the corpse. First with his left hand and then with the right after the razor – its blade still darkly wet with blood – was back in the neck pouch.

An opening shot cracked then, the report sounding trivial in the din of the galloping horses, the hurtling wagon, the snorts and hoofbeats of the mounts with men in the saddles and the cries and curses of the riders as they strove to control the panicked animals. Edge, silent now and with an ice cold grin of triumph curling back his lips from his clenched teeth and narrowing his eyes to the merest slivers of glinting blue, was already hunched low in the seat: using the reins only to steer the team, for he knew the animals were incapable of being driven to greater speed. And so he did not alter his posture on the seat of the jolting and swaying rig as this first shot cracked toward him a bullet that missed by a wide margin.

Nor did he snatch a glance over his shoulder perhaps two seconds later when a whole fusillade of shots exploded a claim to predominance over all other sounds – as mounts and men were calmed in the wake of terror and shock. These shots fired in as hurried a manner as the first one: from guns in the hands of men who were gripped by varying emotions as powerful as that which had triggered Edge's killing move.

But the half breed under the influence of a not-to-be-denied fury retained control over his deadly skills – or perhaps such skills operated automatically in certain situations. And functioned like a standby machine which was switched on to deal with the target for his rage when that target angered him to the point where he lost conscious control of himself. Whichever, he was again in full conscious possession of his thinking processes and abilities for physical actions as the bullets cracked through the air above and to either side of him. Knew he had to remain a clear target on the seat of the speeding rig to have a chance of reaching the relative safety of Elgin City. And aware that the men shooting at him – twelve farmers and one storekeeper – could not possibly share his instinct to kill coldly when apparently

124

crazed by rage. And so the men, firing their revolvers and rifles from the backs of horses spurred to gallops, were reacting impulsively out of high emotion – whether it be dismay or anger or grief or hatred. Thus were more likely to trigger a fatal shock by luck than expert marksmanship. And in such a hell-for-leather situation on an open trail, Edge could do nothing more than trust to luck.

Which was not a state of affairs he relished and so the short lived grin of triumph became a scowl as the hail of bullets sped on ahead of the buckboard and the crackle of gunfire ended: and for stretched seconds Edge could hear only the beat of hooves, rattle of wheelrims and creak of timbers. Then was about to glance over his shoulder – to see if the actual matched with the image that was imprinted in his mind. Of the bunch of riders reining their mounts to an abrupt halt, the rifleman among them preparing to take careful, rock steady aim at the target from bases that were now stationary. But instead, he did a double take at the scene ahead of him. A quarter of a mile along the trail and closing by the moment.

First there was a single gleam of light that was momentarily blurred because his head had been moving as he made to look behind him. But then, as it came into sharp focus, so did many others: and within a second the entire length of Elgin City's main street was ablaze with light. Shafting from each undraped window and open door of every building.

The brilliant illumination emphasised the eerie emptiness of the broad street on which not even a dust devil moved in the pre-dawn hours of the still night. Until Edge, committed to a course of action, drove the buckboard with no slackening of pace past the marker and into town. But even then the sound and movement of the hurtling rig with two horses hauling it and two trailing behind and a living and a dead man up on the seat comprised the only visible noise and activity within Elgin City.

Until another barrage of gunfire exploded. But this time no bullets cracked in the direction of Edge. Hooves beat at the ground but the riders were not in pursuit of the buckboard. Voices were raised, bellowing in the tone of command or shrieking in anger and dismay. The sounds fading in the ears of Edge relative to the distance he travelled along the street. For this new eruption of violence was staged out on the trail and to either side of it. And it was not a running battle.

Then, along both sides of the street, people stepped dispiritedly on to the thresholds of the brightly lit buildings: some to scowl balefully at the racing wagon, others to watch it with indifference or resignation and a few ignoring it to peer anxiously through the settling dust in its wake at the gun battle in the moonlit night to the east of town.

Just one man smiled and raised a hand in welcome – Earl Gray who leaned his broad back against the front of the gallows platform on the courtyard formed by the law office and gaol at the rear and the church and bakery to either side, the lantern with which he had signalled for the lights of Elgin City to be lit still clutched in one pudgy, many ringed fist.

Then the rig was beyond the mid-town area and Edge began to haul rhythmically on the reins to bring the team gradually out of the gallop. And the animals, the foamy lather of sweat gleaming on their coats in the bright light, responded immediately: more amenable to being calmed because the crackle of gunfire had now ceased. So that when the buckboard finally came to rest, almost at the extreme western end of the street, the snorting and wheezing of the nearly exhausted horses were the only sounds to be heard above a distant murmuring of many voices. Until the freckle faced and bald headed Sam Gower stepped across the sidewalk out front of his undertaking parlour and said:

'If Gerry Saxon is as dead as he looks, I appreciate you takin' the trouble to bring him all the way down to me, mister.'

'Was no trouble, feller,' Edge replied as he interrupted his survey of the scene at the far end of the street and realised he had rolled the buckboard to a halt right outside Gower's premises. 'Accident.'

'What happened to the deceased wasn't, I'd say,' the mortician answered as he stepped down on to the street and stooped to look into the blood run face of Saxon whose head lolled off the side of the seat. 'You put pay to just the one?'

He surveyed the empty rear of the rig as if he expected to see other corpses there.

'They all asked for it, feller,' the half breed answered as he swung down from the buckboard and moved alongside it to unhitch the reins of his mount from the rear. 'But Saxon was talking so much garbage, him it was hard to refuse.'

Twelve

THE bay gelding was as fatigued and sweat run as the team horses and the mount of Gerry Saxon by the fear triggered gallop, so Edge did not swing up into the saddle after unhitching the reins. Instead, led the animal by the bridle into a turn along the street toward the mid-town intersection. While behind him the Elgin City undertaker worked with the inherent reverence of a man in his business to lift the corpse down from the seat of the buckboard and carry it into his parlour. And to either side of the half breed and his horse other citizens divided their attention as they remained on or stood just outside the thresholds of the buildings: sometimes eyeing the lone man ambling along at the side of his horse toward where the grossly fat Earl Gray had advanced on to the centre of the intersection, but more often peering up the street to where a large number of men – and some women – were riding their horses in off the east trail. Most of them advancing in the formation of an arc that stretched from one sidewalk to the other, riding to the cadence of a soundless death march with revolvers or rifles drawn and aimed at the group of men bunched dejectedly in front of them.

In the line of captors were Pearl Irish and her four daughters, Chris Hite and Sam Tufts and some other hard men Edge either recognised from yesterday or had never seen before. Only the physically ill-assorted Laura, Anne, Joy and Gloria Irish display-ed broad grins of triumph: while their mother and the hard men appeared to be in sour moods, like they were aggrieved by the chore of guarding prison-ers who could more easily have been killed.

The captives included Irwin Kansler, Prentice Gil-more, Seth Corey and Clay Averill. Plus six others to who the half breed could not put names. So Ray Washington, Charlie Bonham and one other de-posed homesteader had not survived the ambush. Of those who had surrendered to a numerically superior force that was also vastly more experienced at gun-fighting, only the black beared Irwin Kansler was able to emerge from the slough of his despair to lift his chin off his chest, glower at Earl Gray and then inject a larger measure of venom into his expression when he looked beyond the man to snarl at Edge:

'So the bastard didn't buy you, uh? But I gotta say one thing for you, Edge. To set us up that way sure took guts. And I'd like to see the kind you got – spillin' outta a friggin' hole in your belly!'

The fat man, dressed as he had been for dinner at the big house on the hill but with the silver buckled gunbelt supporting the holstered Tranters around his waist again, turned his head back and forth to watch both the half breed and the homesteader with just a hint of a satisfied smile in his wide apart dark eyes and the set of his lips above the series of chins. Then concentrated on the entire bunch of captives as he ordered:

'Hold it right there, runts!'

He draped a hand over the ivory decorated butts of his matched revolvers and the prisoners immediately reined their mounts to a halt: their leader as much infected by the fear of sudden death as the rest of them. And there was a venting of shock by many of the witnesses along both sides of the street: but this was largely masked by the hard men and women peace officers stopping their horses and swinging down from the saddles. Each booting a rifle or holstering a revolver – confident of the fat man's control of the situation. And the smile on the fleshy face of Gray broadened as he accepted the responsibility with uninhibited pleasure in the fact of command.

'Just for the record,' he went on less forcefully, 'Edge knew nothin' of the reception I planned for you people. I've been kept fully informed of – '

He broke off and switched his gaze from the prisoners who were starting to be intrigued by what Gray said, to Edge: and the smile was displaced by an apprehensive frown as he watched the half breed go on by him at the same easy pace, to halt in front of where the bespectacled, sallow complexioned Prentice Gilmore sat his horse on the right of Kansler.

'What's the idea, Joe?' the fat man demanded.

And the Irish women and the hard men grew tense as hands inched toward holstered revolvers.

'You still have my pistol in your pocket, feller?' the half breed asked evenly.

The feed and seed store owner opened his mouth to speak, but anxiety kept his throat constricted. And he simply nodded once then, when the brown skinned hand was extended toward him, he put a hand in his pocket. The tension remained high and seemed to have a palpable presence in the pre-dawn atmosphere. But only Gilmore drew a gun, gripping it around the barrel with a hand that trembled, to extend it butt first toward Edge. Who took it with a brief nod and a soft spoken:

'Much obliged.'

A sigh was vented from many throats and feet were shuffled and rumps moved in saddles as the half-breed brought the Frontier Colt down toward his holster. But this sound of a mass exhalation of breath was not sufficiently loud to cover the thumbing back of the hammer to those in the immediate vicinity. And everyone in Elgin City heard the single crack of the Colt exploding a bullet. Which blasted from the muzzle on a rising trajectory, going under the neck of Gilmore's horse to enter the head of Irwin Kansler via his compressed lips which had tightened as he realised he was to be the victim of the glint eyed half breed.

The bearded homesteader was rocked backwards by the impact of the bullet from close range. Was rigid for a moment as he died, his booted feet trapped in the stirrups. Then, his mouth gaping wide to torrent blood from the hole in its roof, he fell forwards and sideways. To crash to the street between his own and Gilmore's horses: both animals jittery from the shot and ensuing taint of gunsmoke. But not inclined to bolt when there was just an uproar of voices rather than a barrage of other shots in the wake of the new killing. While Edge pushed open the loading gate to extract the spent case and then reloaded the chamber.

The babble of talk was ended with the suddenness of the gunshot that had caused it. And as the half breed slid the Colt into the regular resting place of his holster, Earl Gray said in a dictatorial tone:

'If you weren't Josiah C. Hedges, you'd be dead, mister!'

Edge turned just his head to meet the glowering stare of the obese man with a level and unblinking gaze that tacitly urged Gray to elaborate. At the same time as it expressed a total lack of anxiety that the multi-ringed hands of the Elgin City mayor were now fisted around the butts of the Tranters.

'Worth gettin' yourself in a spot where you could be killed, Joe: just to spite a man who made a monkey outta you?'

'Kansler had this feller steal from me,' Edge answered evenly, with a gesture of his head toward Prentice Gilmore. 'I live by the gun and so, yeah, it's worth risking my life to blast anyone who robs me of it.'

It took several seconds after the half breed had finished talking for the fat man to draw far enough back from the precipice of his volcanic rage so that he could unclench his fists from the revolver butts and get an expression that approximated a smile spread on his tanned, much lined features. When he nodded and allowed:

'I can understand that, Joe. But I'm real glad you didn't blast the man that did what Kansler told him. Wouldn't have been able to give you one last chance then. Come on over to where you belong, Prentice.'

He motioned with his head and the storekeeper, eyes blinking fast behind the lenses of his spectacles and both hands trembling now, swung hurriedly out of his saddle. And jerked viciously on the reins to urge his horse forward: away from eight surviving homesteaders whose combined malevolence directed at the traitor to their cause seemed to be physically bearing down upon the man – to shrink and stoop him.

'Go see Eve if you don't have no objection, mayor?' Gilmore said thickly, and moved even faster after the fat man nodded his approval.

Then Gray told the bitterly resentful group of mounted men who continued to stare toward the departing Prentice Gilmore:

'So it'll give you runts somethin' to occupy your minds while you're kickin' your heels in the gaolhouse. Waitin' to face me. Wasn't Joe sold you down the river. Guys like Joe and me and Zach and the men who're really men, they don't have to sink so low as to . . . hey, where the frig you think you're goin'?'

His tone got shriller and the words were coated with extra venom as he broke off from what was a speech to the whole town to address himself exclusively to the half breed. Who had started along the street again, leading his horse around the bunched prisoners and then on a straight course for a gap in the arc of armed men and women between the squint eyed, tobacco chewing Sam Tufts and the skinny Joy Irish. But when the question was asked, Tufts side stepped to close the gap, showing his stained teeth in a grin: and raised his left arm to run it across his chin and wipe away the tobacco juice which spilled from a corner of his mouth. While the female deputy with a badge pinned to the uncontoured front of her shirt turned sideways on to the half breed who came to an easy halt ten feet away from her. The smiling Tufts was as casual as Edge appeared to be, while the woman adopted a gunfighter's crouch and spread a challenging glower across her thin, angular features as she rasped:

'Granddaddy asked you a question, mister.'

In back of where the tense deputy and the self assured tobacco chewer stood, the brightly lit main thoroughfare stretched to the far side of Elgin City: flanked by uninvolved but far from disinterested citizens who stood like dejected, low ranking sentinels on the sidewalks, stoops and the street. Far from happy with their lot, but disinclined to move against the power and authority of the fat man in order to change things. Or even to assist those who did dare to fight for the rights of freedom. Were merely curious to see the outcome of any such act of defiance while they harboured faint hope of events ever turning circumstances to their favour. And so there was no resentment directed toward the only hard man who was not with Earl Gray now, as he peered at the distant horizon where the dark sky was showing the first streaks of light to announce the approach of the new dawn: just vacuous inquisitiveness, like they were docile dumb animals waiting to discover if they were to get a new master. Wanting to change but feeling helpless to influence the end result.

'I heard him, lady,' Edge told Joy Irish. 'But I figure that even if I knew where I was headed, it'd be my business.'

'Granddaddy!' the flat chested, almost hipless deputy sheriff shrieked eagerly. 'You want me to take him in for talkin' back to you that way?'

'Girl, if you don't wanna a hole in you where a female ain't supposed to have a hole, you won't try it!' her mother warned in a monotone.

'Do me a favour, Joe?' Earl Gray asked with no hint of anger in his voice – as Joy Irish seemed to collect all that had got away from him: and expanded it.

Edge shifted his impassive gaze away from the glowering face of the deputy to look over his shoulder at the fat man. Who stood, his heavily fleshed face displaying an expression that came close to being imploring, beyond the crumpled corpse of Irwin Kansler and the group of mounted men scheduled to die soon.

'Stick around and watch the show,' Gray responded to the quizzical look that paid a brief visit to the lean, dark bristled face of the half breed. And the soft spoken words caused certain of the prisoners to shudder – one to moan softly. 'Clean yourself up some, maybe eat breakfast. Before you leave us.'

'And if I say no thanks?'

'It'd be the wrong thing to say, Joe. Be your last chance outta the window. I'd regret it for the rest of my natural, but I'd have to give the word for you to die, Joe. Matter of principle. As leadin' citizen of this town I can't make exceptions to the rules on account of personal concerns. What d'you say, Joe?'

Sam Tufts ran a sleeve across his smiling, juice spilling mouth. The square faced, mean eyed, scowling Chris Hite directed a globule of saliva at the street. The other hard men tensed to turn and crouch and draw. Pearl Irish seemed to be trying not to show an anxious frown, while all of her daughters grinned. And Joy was unable to suppress a short lived giggle. Edge raised a hand to his jaw and rasped the palm over the stubble of a day and almost an entire night. Said:

'No choice, so no sweat.'

And the gathering tension was abruptly dispersed: only Earl Gray and Pearl Irish content with the anticlimax. Everyone else on both sides of the fence – and those who straddled it – poured tacit contempt and resentment toward the half breed.

'Lock up the prisoners, girl, and have them pick their partners!' the fat man ordered. 'Show'll start at sun up! You men roust out any folks that are still pretendin' they're asleep.'

Amid the sudden noise and activity in the wake of Gray's commands, Tufts said to Edge: 'That skinny-ribs is likely disappointed you didn't put another hole in her, Mac. On account of them she's already got must be near wore out. The way she puts herself around for anybody that don't care there ain't too much meat on the bone.'

The squint eyed tobacco chewer was grinning broadly again, his earlier disappointmet quickly forgotten as he savoured the prospect of the carnage to come.

'Following in the footprints of her grandpa, uh?' Edge said as he tugged on the bridle of the gelding to turn the horse around.

'Uh?' Tufts grunted, bewildered.

'Another town mare, feller.'

The hard man frowned a second longer, then shrugged and shook his head: having failed to make the connection and unworried by it.

Edge tossed over his shoulder: 'That anyone can get to ride.'

Thirteen

THE old, grey haired, wizened facedan attired in a starched white coat who ran the public bath house said that he was called Pop by everybody. He kept apologising for the need to charge a dollar for a hot tub that should only cost five cents while he started the fires in three stoves and then was unnecessarily busy with tending to them as they heated up large pots of water.

The half breed acknowledged the introduction and the first apology, but thereafter ignored the nervously overactive and reedily garrulous bath house attendant. Stood on the threshold of the building's anteroom, his back to the trio of centrally sited stoves, the lines of chairs against each side wall and the doors to the cubicles at the rear. Smoking a cigarette as he surveyed the street that was almost deserted again: but for his gelding hitched across the sidewalk from him and Sam Gower who was leading a horse back toward his parlour from the mid-town intersection – the corpse of Irwing Kansler draped limply over the animal, arms and legs swinging laxly.

The entire sky was a slate grey hue now and there were no longer any pinpricks of starlight visible. The moon was a lighter shade of grey, closing on white.

Just a few lamps were still burning, but for the benefit of the occupants of the buildings rather than to spill light out into night on the brink of day. Chimneys other than that on the roof of the bath house were curling smoke into the chill air of the fall morning.

Edge had needed to relight his cigarette frequently since he started to watch the street empty under the lightening sky. For he was too withdrawn while he concentrated on the decision he would shortly have to make to be aware of present external inconsequentials. Just occasionally became conscious of his surroundings – as if to run a check that his sixth sense for danger did not let him down. At such times, relit his cigarette, heard what the old man was muttering, saw the changes that had come about on the street and noticed how much progress the breaking of day had made.

Thus knew, when he saw the town's undertaker heading up the street with the body of Kansler slung over the back of his horse, that this was the last of the dead to be taken to the funeral parlour – for now. Had seen Gower go earlier out to the east trail, and return leading three corpse burdened horses. Bonham, Washington and a third man whose name Edge could still not recall.

Which was of no consequence. Just as it was of no consequence what the freckle faced Gower said as he drew level with the bath house entrance. But the man's voice coincided with the half breed's train of thought reaching the end of the line and he asked as he used yet another match on the quarter smoked cigarette:

'How's that, feller?'

'I said it looks like it's gonna be another fine day,

138

mister,' Gower answered. And jerked a thumb up at the cloudless sky.

Edge nodded. 'For business, too.'

'Tub's ready for you, sir,' the old timer announced from a steam filled cubicle.

'I ain't ashamed of doin' a necessary job,' the mortician countered evenly – and yet paradoxically pointedly – as he went on by.

And Pop emerged from the billowing steam cloud to say, breathless from the exertion of toting heavy pots of scalding water: 'It's all ready for you to get washed up, sir.'

'I don't do something about it, I could be that already, old timer,' Edge murmured as he tossed the cigarette out on to the street and swung around, features expressionless and tone of voice indicating he was preoccupied.

But he was simply withdrawn from the plane of the present circumstances now. Not rapt in tortuous thoughts, even though he paid no attention to what Pop said to him as he moved across the room between two of the stoves and accepted with a curt nod of acknowledgement the two towels and a cake of soap that were handed to him. Then stepped into the ten feet by four feet steam filled cubicle and closed the door behind hin: slid the bolt across its fixings.

This the opening series of moves in an action that was planned to cut cleanly across or through all the inconsequentials. With the sole objective of re-establishing the self respect he had lost during those brief moments when he submitted to the will of the fat man. The pride he was forced to swallow then had posed a greater threat of making him sick to his stomach than when the homesteaders had made him much more of a prisoner. For while he was determined at the outset to kill – at least – the leader of the bunch for forcing him to do something against his will, he had respect for the men, what they were doing and their motives for doing it. The eruption of the rage that drove him close to insanity was triggered when his esteem for the men abruptly ran out: and there was a strong chance that he was going to be murdered out of hand.

'Sun'll be up any moment now, sir!' Pop yelled. 'Folks are already gettin' hustled out on to the street. Like to go out of my own accord, if you don't mind?'

The old timer had refilled the pots and struggled with them back on to the stoves while Edge stood in the windowless cubicle, swirling the towels around in the hot water and occasionally slapping the surface with the flat of his hand. To make the sound effects of a man taking a bath while steam from the cooling tub lessened but that coming over and under the door from the heating pots increased.

'No sweat, feller,' he called, and heard the old timer's footfalls receding to the doorway, directly opposite the cubicle where the half breed was supposed to be in a tub.

Pop's footfalls rang on the sidewalk and then he stepped on to the street surface. Edge was on the chair set against the right side partition wall by then. And before his straining ears caught the scrape of a more cautious step on the sidewalk boarding, he had swung up and over the partition: between the two feet gap from its dusty top to the ceiling. And had lowered himself to the floor of the next cubicle when the intruder moved over the threshold into the bath house, unimpeded by the door for the old timer had not closed it.

The cubicle in which the half breed now stood, his

back pressed into the corner of the front and side partitions – an inch away from the gap of the part open door – was just as steamy as the one he left, despite the fact that its tub was dry. And maybe the high humidity of the atmosphere was largely responsible for the sweat beads that oozed from the dirt grimed pores of his face and hung stickily in his bristles. But some cause had to be attributed to the tension he felt coiling within him as he listened for other tell-tale sounds to mark the slow and cautious progress of somebody moving from the doorway of the building toward that of the cubicle in which Edge had bolted himself.

But it was difficult to hear anything because of the angrily boiling water in three pots on the stoves. Although this worked to the advantage of the half breed, too – made it impossible for whoever was out in the anteroom to realise there was a suspicious silence existing in the supposedly occupied cubicle.

Not just one person was advancing on the cubicle – then coming to a halt immediately in front of the bolted door. Two people. One hissing:

'Now!' as the other drew in a sharp, hushed breath. The both of them women, which did not alter the moves Edge made as a booted foot crashed against the door of the next cubicle: to tear the screws of the bolt out of the timber and provide shattering entrance for the intruders.

Women or men, young or old, fence sitters or committed to one side or the other. All of them had contributed directly or indirectly to his humiliating surrender in the middle of the brilliantly lit town. And whether they had actually witnessed his back down or not was of no consequence. For he had long ago ceased to care what others thought of him. Only

141

what he was in his own estimation mattered to him.

And it was his opinion in hindsight that he should have called the bluff of the fat man. Taken the risk of Earl Gray meaning what he said. And if he lost, then drilling a bullet deep into the despotic man mountain before the barrage of gunfire from all around cut him down.

But there was no *if* about it. He would have lost and as he stood out on the intersection with every eye fixed upon him and every ear attuned to catch his response, he had never been more certain of anything in his life before. Because Earl Gray's reputation as a ruler of his domain was on the line and a man who had to bluff only did so from a position of weakness. And this man could not allow himself to be seen as weak in front of a townful of people whose free will he had brought with money and who equated wealth with power. Not even to spare the life of a man he did genuinely wish to help. A man he admired as he had admired no other since he lost his revered son-in-law. Until that moment when he forced Edge to back down. And in so doing saved both their lives: but at the same instant was created a virulent contempt at the very opposite end of the emotional spectrum from the feeling he had nurtured for the man previously.

The deputy who had crashed open the door was the youngest, shortest and most heavily built of the Irish sisters: Anne. Who was the closest of the pair to Edge as he swung out of the cubicle doorway, and chopped viciously down on the wrist of her gun hand with the heel of his hand. She vented a cry of pain as her fingers sprang open and the Army Colt was released. A sound which altered tone to one of naked terror as the damaging right hand of the half breed was withdrawn and his left streaked across to fasten on her throat. She choked and clawed with both her hands at his that gripped her. Her revolver clattered to the floor and she was forced to go forward, through the doorway into the cubicle. And slammed into her skinny sister, Joy. Whose Colt was still in the holster as she turned in response to the cries and scuffling sounds – the meat cleaver she had intended to bring down on to the man supposed to be in the bathtub still held high above her head in a two handed grip.

Her thin face with its many angles and hardly any curves was a mask of hatred and it was probably an obscenity rather than a mere scream she intended to vent from her gaping mouth. But then she started to topple sideways from the impact of the collision with her sister as she half turned. And uttered just a low moan of alarm as she was tripped over by the end of the tub, abandoned her hold on the cleaver and flailed her arms in a vain attempt to retain her balance. Then grabbed at Anne to try to stop herself from falling.

Edge reached his free hand around the choking Anne to clench it as a fist in the red hair under the rear brim of Joy's hat. And took a forward step, thrust both arms out at full stretch and leaned from the waist. He glimpsed their faces as they glimpsed his through the constantly shifting clouds of thick, hot steam. The sisters showed matching masks of terror, while the sweat beaded features of the half breed expressed merciless impassiveness. So that the women knew without doubt, as their heads and torsos were plunged into the no longer scalding water, that the man was resolved to kill them.

Just as they had intended to kill him.

They struggled instinctively in the manner of any-one drowning, but the confined space within the tub restricted their efforts. While Edge, up to his sheep-skin coated arms in the water, maintained his iron grip on the throat of one sister and the hair of the other; to force their heads hard against the bottom. His own head turned to peer over a shoulder into the swirling curtain of opaque steam. Prepared to re-lease the half drowned women only if a new danger materialised in the cubicle doorway.

Then water ceased to slop over the sides of the tub as the sisters got weaker. And their struggles faltered to a complete stop – the lithely built Joy outlasting Anne by perhaps five seconds. Only then did Edge straighten up and let go of the throat and the hair. And dried off his hands on an unsodden length of towel as his two victims remained on the bottom of the tub: wedged there face to face, their heads con-cealed by their hats which floated on the surface of the now still and crystal clear water.

The fires in the stoves continued to crackle and the water that boiled in the pots bubbled and sometimes splashed, to hiss angrily on hot metal, as Edge emerged from the cubicle. Stepped on the discarded meat cleaver and nudged the fallen revolver as he ran the towel over his sweat beaded face. Then froze with the towel so positioned he was able to peer over the top of it at the two figures which loomed out of the vapour no more than a yard in front of him. Caught off guard with both hands up to his face but in the split second after the shock of realising this, aware the sixth sense for danger had not let him down. Saw through the blurring, eye stinging steam that the only immediate threat was to Pearl Irish. Who stood totally immobile, her green eyes staring fixedly at the half breed and her mouth slightly open. Like a waxed sculpture of the embodiment of terror. While the much taller and broader figure of Chris Hite who stood slightly behind her to her left expressed a wide grin of pleasure – as though he were the second part of a tableau designed to portray the two extremes of human emotion.

For perhaps a full two seconds the woman sheriff and Earl Gray's top man remained as unmoving as the half breed. And as silent. Then the fat man's daughter started to say:

'You killed my little –'

But her voice was choked off by a rush of blood into her throat which then burst from her suddenly widened mouth: as she leaned forward from the waist. Then went to the side, bent double, after she had slid off the nine inch long blade of the knife in Hite's right hand.

A rifle was gripped in his left hand. And he tossed this toward Edge, who hurled down the towel and instinctively thrust out his hands to catch the weapon.

'Your Winchester, Mac,' Chris Hite said flatly. 'Just took it outta the boot on your saddle. Ready to finish the fight that you started by showin' up around here?'

'I wasn't intending to throw in the towel, feller,' the half breed answered, hooked a booted toe into the sodden fabric and shifted it across the floor. Against the staring eyed face of Pearl Irish where it began to soak up the pool of blood spilled from her gaping mouth. 'Even when I didn't know I had a second to help me clean up the law in this town.'

Fourteen

AGAINST the twin cracks which sounded close to being one as two handguns were exploded on the street, Hite said:

'If I was top hand when you showed up, Mac, it would've been me the fat man fixed for you to gun down. And it could've been me in place of Antrim or Sterlin' or them other two guys that got killed out at the east county line. Ain't no money big enough to keep me on the payroll of a man who sets up his help the way that fat sonofabitch does!'

The smile was gone and the more familiar scowl was in command of the mean eyed square face of the man again. As he punctuated his staccato voiced explanation with a spit and sheathed the knife on the opposite side of his belt from the holster with an Army Colt in it. And retrieved his rifle from where it leaned against one of the stoves.

'Just you figured that?' Edge asked as he moved forward, pumping the action of his Winchester. As, out on the street down toward the mid-town area where the shots had sounded, a man started to plead shrilly for his life to be spared – imploring Earl Gray to believe that he was sorry he had a hand in the doomed attack on Elgin City.

'There wasn't no time to take a vote, Mac,' Hite answered as he turned alongside the half breed.

'Mayor Gray, you runt!' the grossly fat man cut in on the pleading homesteader. 'You give me the title of I'll gut shoot the both of you –'

Again his matched Tranters exploded almost simultaneously. And his bellow of triumph sounded in unison with the report of a shot fired against him. Which obviously missed because he crowed:

'Try to trick Earl Gray, would you? No friggin' chance, sodbuster!'

'Heard the fat man tellin' two of his bitch grand-daughters to come take care of you, Mac,' Hite went on after the interruption of the sounds of violence from outside. 'Then he told me and her to back them up.' He jerked a thumb toward the crumpled up corpse of Pearl Irish, now lost behind the veil of steam as he and Edge drew near to the open door-way. 'Was on the way to here that I figured it out. About Gabe Millard and them other four guys he had killed or let be killed. And now he was fixin' to put pay to you. Hey, better let me check first.'

They were side by side on the threshold of the bath house. The steam here neutralised by the cold air of the brightly sunlit morning. So they were able to see clearly a length of street directly outside the building: totally deserted.

'And you're the only guy he ever had any repect for since Zachary Irish. So if he was havin' you killed, ain't nothin' he wouldn't do if the fancy took him. Seemed to me. So I made up my mind to get the hell out soon as I could. But when I seen you'd turned the tables on them bitches, altered my plan. Like to get outta this town and county knowin' the fat slob ain't around with an axe to grind and money

147

to keep it sharp.'

The fast and toneless talking hard man had barred Edge's exit with the rifle held across in front of him. Now he spat out on to the sidewalk and stepped across the threshold. Shifted the Winchester so that he could raise it and wave it in the air as a signal toward the crowded area of the midtown intersection. This as he displayed his teeth in a smile that only the half breed was close enough to see was marginally away from being a sneer.

'All taken care of, mayor!' he roared.

And Edge, watching intently for Hite to signal him, responded to the unexpected before the man on the outside of the sidewalk had time to make or voice a sign.

'Mayor!'

'Granddaddy!'

'Watch out!'

'He's gonna – '

'You crazy bast – '

'Oh, my God!'

These warnings and pleas and many other shrilly voiced words that sounded less distinctly overlapped and competed for attention. Chorused raucously in the chill air before a gunshot cut across the din and silenced it.

At the same moment Edge emerged from the steamy atmosphere of the bath house: to crack his eyes to the narrowest of slits against the harsh glare of the newly risen sun shafting along the street.

Saw a scene on the intersection that was almost a replica of the one which had been staged when he first rode into Elgin City last night. But with nature instead of kerosene lamps providing the lighting. And certain other, more vital, differences at the centre of the evil tableau.

Four men, roped together in pairs, were already dead: victims of the maniacal fat man's fast drawn Tranters. Edge could put a name to only one of the four – Seth Corey.

Two other pairs of men were roped in the familiar fashion to face up to the obese Earl Gray who insisted upon his hapless opponents matching him in size. Two of the homesteaders with names the half breed could not recall, were forced to stand in front of the gallows: the sour faced Laura Irish holding one by the arm while her pretty sister Gloria maintained a grip on the other.

It was the homesteader named Clay Averill, roped to a helpless man who Edge now recalled as Jacob Astor, who had drawn and fired the Colt loaned by one of the women deputies. To drill a bullet into the enormous bulge of Earl Gray's belly while the fat man had his head turned: distracted by the voice of Chris Hite.

'Shit!' the hard man with a change of heart snarled. 'I wanted to do that personal and –'

The rest of what he said was swamped by the pandemonium that erupted on the intersection. An uproar composed of screams and roars and cries and curses and gunfire and running footfalls. The unarmed, reluctant witnesses to the brutal execution ceremony gone wrong, suddenly whirling to race for cover. Their backs to the centre of the intersection where the hysterically giggling Averill pumped shot after shot into the flabby flesh of Mayor Earl Gray. While his helpless fellow prisoner stared on in horror. And Laura Irish jerked the Colt from her holster and pressed its muzzle to the side of the head of the man she held. Her own head wrenching from

149

side to side to locate the perplexed and shocked hard men – who with a single exception stared at the bullet riddled fat man. Ignoring the woman's bellowed orders or maybe not even hearing her against the bedlam of noise.

The exception was Sam Tufts, who was as shocked and fascinated by the sight of his partner and Edge together on the sidewalk out front of the bath house as were the rest of the hard men by the fact of the multiple wounded Earl Gray remaining on his feet.

Then Tufts flung his rifle to his shoulder, to draw a bead on Chris Hite: who was himself startled into temporary immobility by Gray's incredible endurance. But Edge exploded a shot from the hip, to drill a bullet into the chest of the tobacco chewer, left of centre. And a mess of tobacco sprayed from his mouth as he dropped his rifle and staggered backwards, to collapse and die in the porch of the church.

And Hite died, too, corkscrewing off the sidewalk to sprawl face down on the street: a rapidly blossoming dark stain on the back of his dark vest.

Edge dropped down into a crouch then, and half turned as he pumped the action of the repeater and slammed the stockplate to his shoulder. Raked the barrel to the aim and squeezed the trigger again. To blast a shot diagonally across the street – the bullet finding the chest of the sallow faced Prentice Gilmore. Who had backshot Hite from the doorway of his feed and seed store and who now staggered backwards into his premises. His spectacles flying off his nose as his head jerked in reaction to being shot. And his wife began to wail.

A sound that was suddenly the only one in the entire town of Elgin. For perhaps three stretched seconds as Edge shifted his gaze and the direction of the rifle muzzle toward the mid-town area again.

Where Clay Averill was as horrified as Joseph Astor – the Colt in his hand empty of bullets and no longer aimed at the grossly obese man with six blood blossoming holes in his silk, fringe trimmed shirt front. The two homesteaders trapped between Laura and Gloria Irish were equally stunned by the scene on the centre of the intersection – the man with a gun pressed to the side of his head seemingly less concerned by this than the moves the fat man was making.

To lift his hands and bring them in so that they draped the ivory gripped butts of the Tranters in his holsters. But not with the intention of drawing them against Averill and Astor. For he turned away from the trembling pair of roped together men: shuffling his feet on the street and remaining rigidly upright as if he felt he might fall down and die too soon if he came around any other way.

· Edge straightened up, crossed the sidewalk and stepped down off it while this was happening. And canted the Winchester to his shoulder before he swung out the lever action and folded it back: to drop a discharged cartridge into the dust beside Chris Hite's body and jack a live one into the breech. His cracked eyes never shifted from the scene on the intersection where Earl Gray made the only discernible movements.

Eve Gilmore was now infected by the tension that demanded silence and curtailed her grief stricken wailing.

Edge began to unhitch his gelding from the sidewalk roof support post and Laura Irish shrieked:

'Stay back or I'll blow his rotten head off, creep!'

The reins came free and Edge clucked to the horse

and began to lead him along the street. This as Earl Gray completed his painful turn so that he was facing the half breed, his complexion paled by agony and weakness so that his hair and moustache did not look quite so silvery now.

'Joe don't give a shit for anybody's head but his own, girl!' the Elgin City mayor said, his voice remarkably strong as all the stains on his shirt merged into a single enormous patch of crimson. 'Ain't that right, Joe?'

Edge distrusted certain of the hard men who had now all recovered from their amazement at the turnabout and the stamina of Gray. His ice blue eyes moved back and forth along the narrow tracks between the hooded lids. And his whole apparently relaxed being was poised to retaliate to the first act of aggression against him.

'Anybody's anything, feller,' he said evenly. 'Especially when they make me do something I don't want to do.'

The fat man executed the briefest of nods, like he was afraid a more emphatic movement of his head would upset his balance. 'I know I made a bad mistake when I didn't give you any choice.'

He was within fifty feet of the man who was dying on his feet now. The two pairs of prisoners, the Irish sisters and the eight hard men were all from seventy to a hundred feet away from him when Gray asked:

'My daughter and two of her girls are already . . . ?' He grimaced and rocked in his rigid stance as a bolt of pain seared through his excessively fleshy frame.

'Chris Hite knifed the sheriff and I drowned the deput – '

'Mom!' Laura Irish shrieked. And dragged her

Colt away from the head of the homesteader: brought up her free hand to fist it around the one already clutching the revolver butt. And tracked the gun to aim it waveringly at Edge. Triggered a shot toward the tall, lean, slow walking figure of the impassive half breed. With a negligible chance of hitting the target over such a range with such a gun. And the bullet went high and to the left, to shatter an upper floor window in the front of the Delaware Saloon.

Some of the people crowded into the lower floor bar-room vented their shock in the wake of the crash of glass: and hurriedly withdrew from the windows and batwinged entrance doors.

'You pointed a gun at me once before, lady,' Edge said.

'Mom's dead!' the oldest of Pearl Irish's daughters snarled as she thumbed back the hammer of her Colt. 'And Anne and Joy!'

Despite the powerful emotion that had a firm hold on her, the woman was aware of the ominous circumstances that faced her – the Colt was useless and the man at who she had fired it intended to avenge the act. And she snatched a look at her sister, who had already streaked a hand to her holster to grab at air. Only then recalled with horror that it was her sixgun Clay Averill had used to pump bullets into the massive form of her grandfather.

Laura abruptly remembered this, too. And now raked her anger and fear filled gaze over the hard men scattered across the intersection. All of them with handguns in their holsters and the experience and skill to judge when Edge would be close enough to be within range. Two carried rifles which did not yet threaten anyone. ·

'A thousand dollar bonus for everyone that draws against him!' the woman deputy roared.

And Edge came to an unhurried halt now. Dropped his right hand away from the reins so that it hung close to the jutting butt of his holstered Colt. While his left fisted a little more tightly around the frame of the Winchester canted to his shoulder. Only the Army Colt in the now rock steady grip of both Laura Irish's hands was aimed at him. But every eye was on him, the study overt by the people on the street and surreptitious by those who had fled into the flanking buildings. The fully risen sun took just a little chill out of the air that smelled of smoke from the chimneys of the bath house.

'Can you top that offer, mister?' a blond headed gunslinger with a knife scar along his jaw asked flatly.

The mayor of Elgin City, looking not tanned at all now – almost dissipated by the strain of staying alive on his feet, managed to force out: 'I'm the only one around here buys men!'

'Seems to me you got outbid on Chris Hite, Mr Gray,' a short, stockily built hard man who at fifty plus was the oldest of the bunch growled. And spat in the way the dead top hand used to.

Earl Gray looked questioningly at the half breed, who supplied evenly:

'Gabe Millard, Cleve Sterling, Jesse Antrim and the other two fellers that got killed at the east county line. Maybe Bob Lowell, too.'

'So?'

'A bunch of corpses.'

'What's those guys got to do with anythin', mister?'

Edge waited until the hard men's rasped queries

154

had dried up. Then growled as he shifted his sun glinting gaze over the intrigued face of every hard man and ended the survey on the sick looking countenance of the painfully suffering Gray: 'Hite figured he'd sold only his life to the fat man. And that there wasn't any money big enugh to buy the time and manner of his death.'

'What the frig is that suppose to – '

'The Mayor pays us high but reckons our lives ain't worth that,' the scar faced man cut in on the oldest one. And clicked the thumb and small finger of his gun hand. Then nodded.

'You creeps!' Laura Irish screamed, and lunged forward as she squeezed the trigger and cocked the hammer of her gun. Sprinting toward and aiming at Edge.

Who allowed her just this second wild shot before he brought the Winchester down from his shoulder: and fired it in a one handed grip from his hip. Blinked once in response to the report and again worked the lever action of the repeater as he canted it back up to his shoulder. By which time the woman had been halted in her tracks alongside the fat man, the Colt slipped from her hands as they fell to her flanks. Then her head drooped as if she tried to look at the blood letting hole in her chest, but maybe died before she saw it. And fell hard to her knees, then tipped forward in sight of her grandfather. Who moved his dark eyes just briefly to look at the woman.

Only the surviving Irish sister made a sound – gasped out her pent up breath as she corkscrewed to the ground in a faint.

'You reckon the thought of comin' into all the money was too much for her?' a gunslinger asked.

155

And turned his back on the centre of the intersection to go toward the office of the Elgin County Herald.

'I don't work for no woman!' another growled and went in the wake of the first.

'Especially no slip of a girl like she is!' the oldest hard man added. But held back from leaving the street as he and a lot of other people saw Earl Gray's lips move as the fat man struggled to say something.

The two pairs of roped together homesteaders were behind the dying man, so were not in a position to see his wan, excessively fleshy face. And Jacob Astor spoke first. Asked:

'Won't one of you men please cut us loose?'

The scar faced hard man rasped sourly: 'Nothin' is for nothin', sodbuster. And I don't do nothin' for pretty pleases!'

Earl Gray now managed to find his voice, as his head tilted forward, making his series of double chins more prominent than was usual. Stared down at his elongated, early morning shadow and complained:

'It's gettin' dark. Light the lamps, you runts.'

'The fires'll be burnin' real bright where you're goin', fat man!' a woman shrieked from within the crowded meeting hall.

This as Edge, still watching and waiting for the first sign of a move against him, backed away to get alongside his gelding. And reached across the saddle to slide his rifle in the boot – not pushing forward the hammer until the muzzle was in the leather.

The mayor of Elgin City was rocking back and forth again now. Still rigid except for his lolling head. The jewels in the ring settings on his pudgy hands draped over the holstered Tranters glittering brilliantly in the sunlight with each small movement.

156

And, also with each small movement, a tiny spurt of fresh blood appeared at the bullet holes to add to the great stain which stretched from the shirt collar to the silver buckled gunbelt.

Edge swung smoothly up astride his gelding. And the fat man caught a glimpse of this out of the corner of his eye. Perhaps was delirious and saw the move as one of aggression. Or maybe was able to think rationally in the midst of his pain – and was determined to stop the man who was responsible for his downfall from leaving his town. And he drew the matched Tranters, his very white teeth gritted with the effort this required. Then altered the expression to a grin as he squeezed the triggers, cocked the hammers, squeezed the triggers again and cocked the hammers. Blasted two shots with each gun and then died as he was about to explode two more. And fell with a rush of expelled air to cover the bullet holes he had drilled in the street just a few inches in front of the toes of this boots. Had not had the strength to level the two guns.

Silence came to Elgin City in the wake of the enormous bulk of its mayor hitting its main street. And lasted only a few seconds before Edge heeled his gelding into a slow walk and the hard men moved off the intersection. And not until the gunslingers were all in the newspaper office and the half breed was well advanced along the eastern stretch of the street, did the townspeople emerge into the sunlight.

There was Pop, the white coated bath house attendant, Wiley Reece who rented wagons, the preacherman, Fred Garner the saloon owner and Indian expert who used to walk out with Pearl Irish, Joshua Morrow the banker and Horace J. Hargrove the doctor. And Eve Gilmore, a scared new widow,

Devine with the thick lensed glasses from the livery and Sam Gower, the undertaker.

Some of these and many others continuing to be resentful of Edge who had been forced by the power of circumstances to change things for all time in their community. But who could tell if it would be for the better or for the worse now that they could determine their own future instead of being ruled by the fat man in the big house on the hill? Even the freed homesteaders who had taken a hand in the ending of Earl Gray's tyranny had only hope in what was to follow the brand new dawn. Just as did those other citizens who clustered around them, pumping hands and thumping backs.

Edge rode out beyond the marker sign and lit the cigarette he had rolled. Nobody shouted at him on this occasion and he did not turn around for a final look at Elgin City which had given him nothing for his time there – unless it be a strengthening of a basic belief. That a man who possessed nothing but his life and desired no more was the only man who was truly free.

He was at the start of the valley that narrowed toward the eastern boundary of Elgin County when he met another lone rider. A mean eyed, thin faced, tension taut man in dark clothing who watched Edge like a prowling animal as they closed. And asked from fifteen feet away:

'There's a charnel house of new dead back by the fence – that mean the man that runs this piece of territory is hirin' on new help?'

'No, feller,' Edge answered as neither he nor the newcomer moved to halt their mounts.

'Reckon I'll check that out for myself, mister,' the grimacing hard man growled. 'Seein' as how I know

Earl Gray from way back and –'

'Go ahead,' the half breed allowed with a slight shrug as his gelding and the stallion of the other man moved slowly on by one another. 'But you'll be flogging a dead horse.'

'I'll need to hear that from Earl myself, mister. Since he owes me a favour.'

'What he figured he owed me,' Edge said. 'From way back. But the old mayor Gray, he ain't what he used to be.'

THE END

NEL BESTSELLERS

T51277	'THE NUMBER OF THE BEAST'	*Robert Heinlein*	£2.25
T50777	STRANGER IN A STRANGE LAND	*Robert Heinlein*	£1.75
T51382	FAIR WARNING	*Simpson & Burger*	£1.75
T52478	CAPTAIN BLOOD	*Michael Blodgett*	£1.75
T50246	THE TOP OF THE HILL	*Irwin Shaw*	£1.95
T49620	RICH MAN, POOR MAN	*Irwin Shaw*	£1.60
T51609	MAYDAY	*Thomas H. Block*	£1.75
T54071	MATCHING PAIR	*George G. Gilman*	£1.50
T45773	CLAIRE RAYNER'S LIFEGUIDE		£2.50
T53709	PUBLIC MURDERS	*Bill Granger*	£1.75
T53679	THE PREGNANT WOMAN'S BEAUTY BOOK	*Gloria Natale*	£1.25
T49817	MEMORIES OF ANOTHER DAY	*Harold Robbins*	£1.95
T50807	79 PARK AVENUE	*Harold Robbins*	£1.75
T50149	THE INHERITORS	*Harold Robbins*	£1.75
T53231	THE DARK	*James Herbert*	£1.50
T43245	THE FOG	*James Herbert*	£1.50
T53296	THE RATS	*James Herbert*	£1.50
T45528	THE STAND	*Stephen King*	£1.75
T50874	CARRIE	*Stephen King*	£1.50
T51722	DUNE	*Frank Herbert*	£1.75
T52575	THE MIXED BLESSING	*Helen Van Slyke*	£1.75
T38602	THE APOCALYPSE	*Jeffrey Konvitz*	95p

NEL P.O. BOX 11, FALMOUTH TR10 9EN, CORNWALL

Postage Charge:
U.K. Customers 45p for the first book plus 20p for the second book and 14p for each additional book ordered to a maximum charge of £1.63.

B.F.P.O. & EIRE Customers 45p for the first book plus 20p for the second book and 14p for the next 7 books; thereafter 8p per book.

Overseas Customers 75p for the first book and 21p per copy for each additional book.

Please send cheque or postal order (no currency).

Name ....

Address ....

....

Title ....

While every effort is made to keep prices steady, it is sometimes necessary to increase prices at short notice. New English Library reserve the right to show on covers and charge new retail prices which may differ from those advertised in the text or elsewhere.(7)